Biography

I0679202

Jack Brutus Penny was born in September 1986 in London, England, and grew up in the north London area. After graduating with a degree in Psychology, he moved to Kanagawa, Japan. Since then he has had a variety of jobs, including that of an English lecturer, a private interpreter, a freelance graphic designer, a writer, and an illustrator. His works, all in the nonsense genre, include volumes from the Riddle Me Collection, In Truth Stories, and The Allegaurus (in editing).

'I find nonsense comes quite naturally to me. Possibly because I have a good grasp of imagination and an even worse grasp of how to communicate it. It also helps that I'm a dyslexic living in Tokyo, so I've forgotten half my English, and the other half I could never spell.'

Excerpt from official website [www.jackbrutuspenny.com] biography page.

In Truth Stories

Jack Brutus Penny

JBP Publishing
First Printing, 2017

ISBN 978-4-908906-02-2

www.jackbrutuspenny.com

For those with inquisitive minds

&

For those that fill them with nonsense

Contents

WHY THE CHAMELEON WEARS
A COAT OF MIRRORS

Colour is such an important thing. Colour can show whether a food is ripe or not, or even whether a food is edible or not, though we surely can't call inedible food 'food'. Colour can also warn us of the dangerous animals we might come in contact with. The yellow Wasp, for instance, has quite poor people skills and can say things that sting a little, suggesting one should avoid yellow. It is not surprising then that our own colour is so important to us. So why, you I'm sure wonder, if colour is such a defining feature, does the Chameleon not have a colour of its own? Why, and how, does the Chameleon just blend? Well, since you have asked such insightful questions, and thus far no outsightful answers have been provided, though this is not surprising as most people can't remember back to when there was no colour, grant me a moment to give you the honest account of how this all came about, just so, in truth.

After the painting of the world, when all life began, and the vault of the sky separated so that the sun and the moon could divide time between themselves fairly, neither being greater or lesser than the other, when plants and flowers bloomed radiant colours, bore fruit bearing seeds, and everything was pretty agreeable, this was when the first animals were born. The first animals had neither colour, not even the Rainbow Fish, nor pattern, not even the Leopard its spots, until they too were painted. But this story happened early on the sixth day when all the animals had been mixed and baked, but no dye or icing had yet been added. All but one. Early on this sixth day, the Chameleon, whilst still being baked, shot out its long, dexterous tongue and scooped up some red and blue and yellow berries so that when it was baked, it came from the oven already glazed a marvellous array of colours.

<One should always observe the sky head tilted to the left, for unattended, that's where the sun and moon are hanging.

However, the Chameleon walked among the other animals as oblivious as a pen in a pencil case – naturally there but unaware how unnatural it was. All the animals would offer kind words, for they were generous and shared a lot with each other.

'What a beautiful coat you have,' they would say. But since the Chameleon had never seen itself, it assumed these were pleasantries of the typical kind and returned the offer.

'What a marvellous jacket you wear,' the Chameleon said to the, then and still, grey Donkey, making the Donkey feel unintentionally though nonetheless intensely like an Ass.

So one day, the greyish-brown and completely monotonous animals gathered and decided something must be done. Since it wasn't any fault of the Chameleon's, they decided to educate it rather than give its tongue to the cat, who collected tongues, though no one knew why, and for some reason, no one bothered to ask. So they invited the Chameleon to a picnic by the lake. It being such a significant moment, all animals of all kind were there for the picnic, though not really for the picnic at all.

The animals were far cleverer than they were colourful, and when the Chameleon arrived, they proposed a game, or rather, a treasure hunt of sorts – the first animal to spot an animal they've never spotted before wins. Despite knowing the purpose of the game, for all the animals except the Chameleon were in on it having proposed it together, they still found the game delightfully amusing and ran around with the Chameleon, not mockingly at all, except the Mockingbird, but it couldn't help itself, pouncing and plunging in all directions.

They were spinning as fast as they could – climbing trees and digging outlandishly deep holes – but no animal approached the water, which sat still, waiting. The Chameleon, also marvellously thrilled, was skipping everywhere, and if the other animals weren't so preoccupied, they'd surely have thought the day successful enough just to see the Chameleon's pleasure.

Eventually, the Chameleon, skipping-tumbled down to the bank of the lake, wishing to confer with the bank tellers, for their stories may tell of some animal it had never spotted before. But it stopped by the water. As its left eye focused intently forward, its right was rolling freely about and noticed something unfamiliar in the water, something as colourful as a tongue-full of berries. The Chameleon looked again, squinting to show that it was trying to focus. There was an animal, clearly ept at swimming, incredibly colourful, despite all the other animals being so greyish-brown and completely monotonous, one the Chameleon had certainly never seen before, squinting right back at it.

'Who's there?' the Chameleon asked, arching its neck back and dipping the edges of its mouth to show how inquisitive it was. But the animal only responded with the same, quite perfectly timed words. 'Who's there?' repeated the Chameleon, hopping back and then leaning over once again, its mouth still dipped. This animal, thought the Chameleon, is the most splendid creature of them all, and the Chameleon, as if pushed, dove unexpectedly into the water to embrace such splendiderouness. Falling through the water, the Chameleon splattered and spluttered and pulled itself back up. As it looked drippingly up, it realised two things – that all the other animals had stopped their search and were lined watching the Chameleon silently, and that the animal it had never spotted before, the only animal with such an array of colour, was itself. All the on-looking animals, for the Chameleon had arched its eyebrows and pursed its lips to indicate it had realised these two things, began to jump and cheer. But little did they know that with one solution comes another problem, for now it was too late, and the Chameleon was in love.

All the colour in the world.

The sun came and went, and it was time for the moon to march the sky, and the Chameleon still sat, near the bank, by the water, looking and squinting. The sun came back from its rest and took its sentinel place, and the Chameleon was still there. The sixth day ended, the seventh even came and went. All the animals now had been properly painted with their colours, especially the Rainbow Fish, and patterns had been given, though the Leopard's spots would come later, and the Chameleon was still there.

Since it wasn't any fault of the Chameleon's, the animals thought, they decided to assist it rather than make it hold its horses, for that certainly would have preoccupied the Chameleon, but horses are cruelly heavy. So the animals thought and thought until they could have thunk no longer and finally came up with a solution. If the Chameleon could always see itself, then it would not have to squint at the water but could at least live an ordinary life, though in love with itself.

So the animals gathered as much Walrus tusk as they could get, of course, donated by the Walrus, for the Walrus was most bitterly contemplative having regrettably lost its little Oyster friends only recently, though that's another story already told, and so its tusks must be incredibly reflective. And from them, the animals made a morse coat of ivory mirrors.

'Chameleon,' the animals pled, 'do wear this morse coat, we made it special for you.' But the Chameleon was so bedevilled with itself that it could neither look at nor listen to anything else. 'Chameleon,' the animals re-pled, 'do wear this morse coat, and then you might see yourself in everything, in spite of eating or playing, and then surely be better.' This the Chameleon gladly heard and took the morse coat of ivory mirrors, swung it over its back, and fastened it firmly, for the Chameleon wanted to be able to see itself in everything.

Unfortunately, with this swing and fasten, the Chameleon suddenly and resolutely disappeared. Not a single wild thing there had considered that such a reflective coat would reflect upon all the surroundings and not just the Chameleon itself. Now, none of the animals could see the colourful Chameleon. They called to the Chameleon, naturally in rhyme for they already had a reason, 'Chameleon, Chameleon, by the lake, won't you come back to us opaque?' but nothing stirred. They called the morse coat, 'Mirrors, mirrors, 'round its chest, won't you give back our friend undressed?' but still nothing stirred. The animals groped and poked and probed high and low, but there is nothing as problematic as finding something unseen, other than possibly being a Sow, since it consists principally of dealing with Boars.

If not looked at the right way, it's not only the Chameleon you won't see. >

Likewise, and to worse effect, the Chameleon could no longer see itself. When the Chameleon climbed a tree, it could only see a tree. When the Chameleon lay on a rock, a rock it could see. And it couldn't see the morse coat of ivory mirrors to unfasten. 'Were I a Ferret with a plain brown coat', the Chameleon bemoaned regretfully, 'or a charcoal Mustang or a Horse of another colour, I would at least have a tinge of my own, as all would say, "Look, there goes the Horse in its appropriate glaze!" But now I am a tiffany mutt, and people will say of those that blend with any crowd with changeable characters and no real stuff of themselves, "Look, there goes a Chameleon in a morse coat," for I, now, have no true colours.'

All illustrations for this story are from original sketches observed on previous trips to this peculiar world. From here on out, or in this book as it may be, most illustrations are postliminary interpretations and as such were given to more fanciful details yet even less verity.

WHY THE TURTLE PUT ON ITS SHELL

If you are reading this account, then you are most likely doing it from a place over which there is a roof of some sorts, unless it is a sunny day, and you are lying on a patch of grass or sitting on a wooden bench with the sound of cars chugging past in the distance or in fact reading this account anywhere without a roof of sorts, though I suspect there will be one. And you may be wondering, or may have before starting to read this account, how convenient it is for the Turtle to have its shell and be able to move anywhere with a roof over its head. Then another thought may have occurred to you that went along the lines of, wait a moment, its shell serves not only as a roof but also as a shield to protect it from children who poke turtles on the beach and do other annoying things too. Notwithstanding my applaud to your inquisitive mind, you are, as it happens, mostly incorrect regarding why the Turtle put on its shell other than the part about other annoying things, which is fairly accurate. So if you, then, were wondering why the Turtle put on its shell if it wasn't for these reasons, assent to my giving the story, and I shall tell you, just so, in truth.

This tale begins in a rather peculiar way, with an ending we are all astutely familiar with, and ends with something we may well be aware of but have even less than a clue as to how it began.

When the famous Dickory Dock welcomed ships made only from hickory trees that bud yellow-green hickory catkins, as the dock was built likewise, and steadfastness was everything, and before the renowned Hickory Clock was erected, neither the Town Mouse nor the Country Mouse had ever visited the area. In truth, the two were equally steadfastly resolute to stay in their respective homes and be generally rather miserable. At this time, the great and wise Dog had not yet deciphered the mysteries of reflections, and woodcutters came either honest and rich or wishing a river did always bring axes. At this time of development and learning, there was one Master Tortoise and one Crackerjack Hare, and they were both, for want of a better word, incredibly obsessed with being better than the other.

By now you must recognise the ending with which this tale will begin, but first some amendments to the tale must be made, as, as with any tale, fable, yarn, allegory, or thereof, the lines between what happened in exactness and what just happened are oftentimes smudged, as if made of more chalk than truth.

So first, the Master Tortoise was younger than most presume, though the confusion is perfectly natural, as it became riddled with wrinkles as a child from staying in the bath too long. Moreover, this Master Tortoise was presently, at that time anyway, the Mayor of the famous Dickory Dock, having left the military early due to a questionable paper cut, which may or may not have just been another wrinkle. And, though it was no significant point then, as the lack of anything rarely is, the Master Tortoise had no shell but a bare wrinkly back to suit its front.

The Crackerjack Hare also was older than most presume and had served in the military as a private along with the Master Tortoise, though had by now, at that time at least, become a Commanding Officer. As the Royal Ruby IV Hickory Frigate was today, at that time, docked at pier thirteen, the Crackerjack Hare was presiding the area to oversea everything.

At this time, at that time, the two would often compete at singing this, eating that, crouching here, or, indeed, running there. And it was well known at this hour, at that time, that the Mayor controlled the local print-press newspaper, which may or may not then have had a bias in its reportings. We can indeed say that the fabled race took place, but other than that, it is difficult to properly determine what happened in truth, and even less is known of what happened following the race, except to those who read this tale in hindsight.

It seems that after the fabled race and with the invention of delivering print-press newspapers to other towns, the Master Tortoise became turfly famous. People and animals and a queer-looking creature with an even queerer sounding name would regularly pester the Master Tortoise until he started having to actually do things in the daytime, and then finally until he disappeared leaving only a note, that read, 'I must go, for I have gotten another paper cut.'

Whether the Master Tortoise had really gotten a paper cut or simply gotten into a lather, trying and failing to cut the mustard, is unknown. Either way, the Master Tortoise had left and was never seen at the famous Dickory Dock again.

The Master Tortoise, pursued by people and animals and, expressly, by a queer-looking creature with a queer sounding name that it could not pronounce for the life of it, was forced to go into hiding. It hid in many places – in crooks, though the scoundrels would themselves run off and leave the Master Tortoise exposed; in nannies, though they were too busy caring for querulous children to conceal it properly; under millstones; and behind chimney tops. The Master Tortoise, in fact, hid anywhere and everywhere it could. The trouble was that having found an adequate dustpan or brush within which to keep, the Master Tortoise would eventually have to reveal itself to stretch its wrinkled legs lest they get so wrinkled they became accordions. You see, the Master Tortoise was not musically inclined at all. In these moments of revelation, a person or an animal or, more often than not, a queer-looking creature that may in fact have simply been wandering around though seemed to be looking for something would spot it, and it would have to find a new place to hide.

One day, though this event only lasted approximately twenty-one minutes, the Master Tortoise marked a fine-looking Snail, sporting a fine-looking coffer on its back, for which it had its own reasons. 'What a fantastic idea,' thought the Master Tortoise, not actually knowing what idea had lead to such a situation, so speaking wildly out of turn. 'I can hide in a box such as that and still stretch my wrinkled legs,' and so the Master Tortoise approached the Snail slowly, mind not due to age or speed limitations but out of timid manners.

'From where did you acquire such a formidable strongbox?' inquired the Master Tortoise, rather too candid for the Snail's liking, but there we are. 'I must have one.'

'Uhghem,' the Snail cleared its throat unintelligibly, for it found speaking to the Master Tortoise arduous and wished to show this. 'This cumbersome trunk,' for it was easily three centimetres across, 'which I must lug every which way I go like a shadow on a cloudless day, was thrust upon me. A fateful buckshot discharged left this shell on my back,' the Snail muttered despondently. 'Curse that Royal Frigate that left this weight on my shoulders.'

'What chance,' thought the Master Tortoise, though it did not say so despite thinking it with quotation marks. In fact, this thought on punctuation occupied the Master Tortoise for a moment, making the Snail's temper even shorter until it was positively minuscule.

'I am in need of such a shell, for I am unjustly hunted by the Crackerjack Hare, the Commanding Officer of the Royal Ruby IV Hickory Frigate.'

'Ha,' scoffed the Snail, cheering up a little. 'How ironic it would be for this shell on my back to help you flee that fateful frigate. If you can take it then I'll give it to you,' offered the unwitting Snail, though in a tone that implied the Snail thought that taking it would be a far more difficult task than a different tone would have implied.

First, the Master Tortoise tried greasing the Snail's palm, but because it was snake oil, and because the Snail's palm was hardly discernible, this didn't help much. So next the Master Tortoise tried breaking the shell. Now breaking a shell isn't like breaking ice. You can break ice with a very soft word, and, in fact, this is preferred, but even hard words generally break no bones, and a shell is much like a bone but not quite the same. So the Master Tortoise took the hardest words it could, and levying them just right, expelled the words directly at the shell's soft spots, which the shell happened to have for milk as do most shells being much like bone though not quite the same. So with the Master Tortoise's hard words against the milk, the soft sound of a crack followed by the sharp sound of a larger crack could be heard, leaving an average-sized crack, which could be seen in the middle, and finally the Master Tortoise used some sticks and stones to prise the shell clean off.

The Master Tortoise slid into the shell, stretching it a little, for he was a little heavier set than the Snail, until it was nice and snug. Now the Master Tortoise was a completely new animal, in appearance, at least, except for its wrinkled legs, which poked out of holes in the shell, leaving little wrinkled clues to its true identity.

This subtle little wrinkled clue glimmered just enough to be dangerously noticeable, so the Master Tortoise knew that it would need to change at least one more thing to be better hidden. It thought quickly, for it knew that it was time to hit the road and had to dress its feet properly first or hitting the road would rather hurt. First, the Master Tortoise considered changing its colour, but in truth, it knew the problems the Chameleon was having and thought better of it.

Then it considered changing its size. How massively grand it would be to shrink to the size of a bee or even grander, the size of a bee's knee, but then it would be too monumentally small to keep the shell it had just laboriously acquired. Then the Master Tortoise thought of changing its name but decided there was too much in a name. Its hand was the hand of the Master Tortoise. Had its name been changed, its hand may no longer be that of its. Its foot, its now subtle little wrinkled glimmered foot, would be a foot unpossessed, for it would no longer be Master Tortoise's foot.

The name that distinguished Master Tortoise from any other was now all it had. All is in a name. How could one tell another to smell the sweet scent of a rose had it no name? But by simply saying the name of a rose, a sweet smell fills the air and mind of the listener, so a thing and its name are inseparable. A rose by any other name, such as a button or teaspoon, could absolutely not smell as sweet. No, the Master Tortoise could not change its name.

But then a clapping and a clamouring came from over the hill and far away, but approached quickly until, to the Master Tortoise's disbelief, a queer-looking creature stood walking before it. The queer-looking creature appeared to be feigning to continue walking straight by but was clearly up to no good and down to some bad while at it, so the Master Tortoise blurted something out before it could pass. 'Something!' blurted the Master Tortoise. Startled, the queer-looking creature stopped, and having given it a good look, the Master Tortoise realised that it, in fact, looked quite normal except for its lack of eyes, for it only had two.

'Did you say something?' asked the Ipieaicoiciki.

'Agh!' the Master Tortoise ejected violently, remembering that indeed it had a far queerer sounding name. The Master Tortoise now entirely panicked blurted from inside its new shell, 'I don't race, and I know not this Mister Tortoise, though I expect it a fine fellow. I'm...' it looked around quickly and saw a myrtle shrub from which delicious blue-violet flavoured tea was made, '...I'm tea...myrtle, t-myrtle, just turtle, and I must be on my way, good day good sir.' With which, the Turtle plucked a myrtle branch as though to show its purpose for coming to this place and took its leaves.

WHY THE PEACOCK PAINTED
EYES ON ITS TAIL

If you ask your mother why the Peacock has eyes on its tail, she might just tell you that the Peacock was born with them, and if she happens to be wiser than most, she might quickly leave the room, as this clearly creates more questions than answers. Why was the Peacock born with eyes on its tail? You might then ask. If she, however, happens to stay in the room and decides to answer, she might tell you that the eyes help intimidate tigers and bears and spinach and lions and big brothers and other dangerous things one would want to intimidate so that they stay away. But still this doesn't answer your question of why, and all of this is a lot of mights. The trouble is, your mother hadn't been born yet when this story began, and neither had your grandmother despite being as old as she is, so it is no fault of theirs that they don't know that, in truth, the Peacock painted the eyes on its tail. Nor is it any fault of theirs that they don't know why. But I do. So, avoiding any inappropriate discussions as to my age, allow me to tell you the tale of what really happened, as it did, just so, in truth.

Long ago, only two years following the building of the Great Rubber Tree Bridge and four years before its unfortunate collapse, hurting another poor ant with such high hopes, when the forests and rivers were not so new but not so old either, there was an animal called the Ipieaicoiciki, and even then, when names were all kinds of odd, it was difficult to pronounce. The Ipieaicoiciki had never had a mate, partly because its unpronounceable name made introductions challenging, and partly because it had never found one. The Ipieaicoiciki would roam the forests but not the rivers, for it couldn't swim all too well, looking for a partner.

One day, when the moon would have been quite beautifully crescent-shaped had it been night, the Ipieaicoiciki was fumbling around muttering to itself, 'how am I to ever find a mate at the speed I am roaming? Clearly I must find a way to search more of the forest but not the rivers, for I can't swim all too well, faster.' Fortunately or un, depending on your mindset, the Ipieaicoiciki muttered with its head hung dejectedly low and was overheard by a passing Bush-tailed Porcupine. In those days, or at least up until two years before the collapse of the Great Rubber Tree Bridge, porcupines had no spines, except for the one inside their back, and beautiful silky fur. But, in truth, that's another story.

'I can search this forest as quick as you can say your name,' said the Bush-tailed Porcupine. 'I crouch down like a cat pretending it's about to pounce but actually being about to suddenly lick the back of its leg', it said while thrusting its leg up to demonstrate, 'and swiftly run through the gaps and holes in the forest roots.' Knowing how long it took to pronounce its name, the Ipieaicoiciki wasn't very reassured by this, but the Porcupine's method did indeed seem quick, and anything was worth a try at this rate. So the Ipieaicoiciki crouched down like a cat pretending it's about to pounce and swiftly made to run through the gaps and holes in the forest roots. Head first the Ipieaicoiciki went but head first catching its crown, and not the princely kind, and then all its other feathers, the Ipieaicoiciki curled into a sticky topknot with plumes this way and twigs that. Had anyone seen the Ipieaicoiciki at this point, they wouldn't have been remiss to think it were hair and hide and nothing in between.

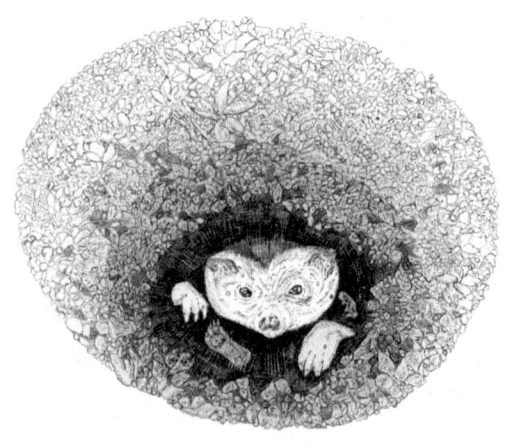

Having untangled itself, the Ipieaicoiciki lay on its back and continued to dejectedly mumble to itself whilst looking distantly, though there is no telling to what distance, at the sky. At this moment, it just so happened that a White-cheeked Partridge flew down and rested in a nearby pear tree, for loving the taste of pears so much, the two are quite inseparable.

'What spoilt pear have you found?' the White-cheeked Partridge asked, looking down. Luckily the Ipieaicoiciki had heard this expression before from its cousin, who was an old Chestnut-breasted Partridge, though it claimed to be a Cork Partridge, so knew what it meant. Now as an aside, you should know that there are many manners and types of partridges – in fact each single partridge seems to prefer its own individual name and to be acknowledged for its own individual characteristics, but all that said, generally a partridge sits in a pear tree, and the expression 'what spoilt pear have you found?' is basically asking what the matter is, for it seems you have a sour expression.

'I am disappointed because I have no partner and cannot search this forest quick enough to find one. I came within a hair's breath of running through the roots of the forest, but the air was too thin down there.'

'Well that is no matter,' replied the White-cheeked Partridge. 'Are you not, as I, a bird? Can you not, as I, but fly from one pear tree to the next? The pears have such a lovely taste after all.'

The White-cheeked Partridge, having gone off topic, and then simply gone off, left the Ipieaicoiciki in thought. It was, at least it believed, a bird but had never flown before. Though, since anything was worth a try, it decided to give it a go. The Ipieaicoiciki backed up a little, bent its knees open as if doing a double-pirouette, for that's how its knees bent, and lurched into the air. Not really knowing how to fly, the Ipieaicoiciki tried the breaststroke at first but fell, thumping, down on its breast. It vaulted a second time and tried backstroke but fell flat on its back. Now, had anyone been there, they wouldn't have been remiss to think it were a spring chicken, though it wasn't as young. The third time the Ipieaicoiciki caprioled into the air, it did the butterfly stroke and thought for a moment it was flying but had, in fact, landed caught in the branches of a great tree, though not rubber or pear. With its first leg pulled up and the last leg down and having no other legs, it was left with no leg to stand on.

The Ipieaicoiciki hung there only for a short while before a troupe of Capuchin Monkeys swang its way, rather obsessed with the New Age, as they called that period. Obviously, the Capuchin Monkeys had not considered how ages are inclined to change with time, and new soon becomes old, so they parted their hair in the latest fashion and only ate insects dipped in Hickory sap from the Dickory Dock, for that's what was done in this new age. Chittering and chattering, they came bustling over and sat or hung or lay or perched or squat, or whatever they could do to all fit on the same branch as the Ipieai-coiciki was stuck in.

'What are you…' began one Capuchin Monkey.

'Hanging in this tree for?' finished another.

The Ipieaicoiciki looked at the two as anyone looks at two who finish each other's sentences, with so much disinterested disdain that you could see its motionless eyes wanted to roll but couldn't be bothered. 'I am trying to search the forest as quick I can for a mate, but alas, I am now stuck stretched in this tree,' replied the Ipieaicoiciki. 'I have tried crouching like a cat pretending it's about to pounce and running through the gaps and holes in the forest roots. I have tried to fly, for I am, at least I believe, a bird, though I've never flown before. And now I am here,' the Ipieaicoiciki lamented bitterly.

'Well I…'

'Never. You won't…'

'Find a mate hanging like…'

'That. Why not – '

'Swing like us?' the Capuchin Monkeys replied in chorus, having clearly not noticed the motionless desire in the Ipieaicoiciki's eyes to roll. Or possibly having noticed it and not cared. But despite everything indeed being worth a try, without hands or feet that could grip, the Ipieaicoiciki quickly checked its feet, but it was certain they were far too feet-like to grip, realised this was a fruitless endeavour.

'I fear I cannot swing. But would you kindly give me a hand to get me out of this pickle?' the Ipieaicoiciki said, realising when it had checked that one of its feet was unceremoniously wedged in a tree-pickle.

'Of course, yes – '

'We can!' laughed the Capuchin Monkeys and immediately began applauding and cheering, which was a very odd spectacle indeed, as the cheers that started somewhere were being finished elsewhere. In fact, it is said that this was the first ever instance of surround sound, and it intimidated the Ipieaicoiciki immensely. But as they did so, the branch shook and jived like a noisy old washing machine, until the Ipieaicoiciki's foot was freed from the pickle and the branches altogether, and it fell to the ground with a thwack.

The thwack, as unpleasant as it was, brought a great idea that had been lurking at the back of the Ipieaicoiciki's head straight to the front. In fact, it did this with such force that the idea jumped to the tip of the Ipieaicoiciki's tongue and straight off so that the Ipieaicoiciki had to reach out and grab it before it was lost. Fortunately, it landed at the tip of the Ipieaicoiciki's toes, for it had no fingers on the ends of no hands, so was easy to catch. This idea was so great that it would solve the two problems faced by the Ipieaicoiciki simultaneously, without the need of a stone or of hurting any birds. Immediately the Ipieaicoiciki got to its feet and dashed for some Hickory sap. The Ipieaicoiciki dipped one of its feathers, using the pickle it was in before as a handle, gently into the dark molasses and proceeded to carefully paint one, two, four, six eyes onto its sweeping, and now a little dishevelled, tail. From then on, the Ipieaicoiciki hopefully and successfully roamed the forest. Then, with its tail high and coated with eyes, it could see over the forest grasses and flowers and right over everything and having found a good mate, introduced itself as thus, 'How do you do? I am the Ipieaicoiciki, but since all my eyes are now on my tail, please call me Peacock,' which was a much easier name to be introduced by.

WHY THE PORCUPINE PUT NEEDLES IN ITS BACK

Ask your biology teacher why the Porcupine has spines, and you'll probably hear some codswallop about natural selection and protection from predators and other curious animals. Ask your chemistry teacher why, and you might hear that the Porcupine spines are made from one of the hardest materials, pound for pound, that they know off. They will probably leave out the fact that they know of very little. Ask your physics teacher why, and you best be prepared to hear of barbed needles reducing penetration force and increasing pull-out force fourfold, all of which is an impressive mouthful but irrelevant. The trouble is not scientific but linguistic. All of these answers tackle the question how but not why. You might get closer to an answer if you asked the Farmer or Postman, who may have tried to pat the Porcupine, confusing it with a black and white cat. However, none truly knows why the Porcupine has spines unless they know the story that explains that eventful day, as I do. So if you don't mind, why not ask me why? And I'll tell you precisely the reason, just so, in truth.

In the seasons when animals spoke quite openly with humans and enjoyed spring and autumn together, though summer was too hot, and winter had not been invented yet, there was a spineless Porcupine. In truth, all Porcupines were spineless then, so were both very soft, like a cotton pad, and oftentimes incredibly cowardly, though this story might seem quite contrary to that. This particular Porcupine was a Bush-tailed Porcupine; however, all Porcupines being rather alike, that doesn't matter much, and we can assume that whatever happened to this Porcupine also happened to the rest, as it surely did.

This Porcupine lived with a mottled Cat and a spotted Dog and kept an older Lady as a pet, even though she had no speckles on her skin at all. Each of the animals cared dearly for the older Lady, for she was quite a lot older, which made her that much more adorable.

Every morning the mottled Cat would kindly wake the older Lady by softly climbing into her bed and calling into her better ear, which was the younger one, having come out at birth a whole one-and-a-half seconds later.

'Dear older Lady, dear older Lady,
It's time to stretch your feet.
Dear older Lady, my dear, it's colder lately,
Let's build the fire's heat,' the mottled Cat would call, and the older Lady would be gently awoken.

To be viewed as if the older Lady, on its side. >

Why the porcupine put needles in its back **41**

At lunchtime, after eating and feeding the older Lady, though they let her prepare her food herself, as she had a discerning stomach and besides, was rather good at preparing food, the spotted Dog took her for a walk. The spotted Dog would fetch her slippers and lead, with which it kindly tied one end around its collar, the other to be placed carefully in the older Lady's hand, for let alone she tended to wander off and would call her from the door.

'Dear older Lady, dear older Lady,
It's time to take a stride.
Dear older Lady, my dear, lest we get lazy,
Let's breathe the air outside.'

And every evening, having gotten the older Lady up and taken her for a walk, the animals would let the older lady relax by knitting in her cosy armchair in the sitting room by the fire. It was at this time that the Porcupine, soft like a cotton pad, attended the older Lady, and what a lot of attending it took. Needles of quite precise shape and length, threads and wools and fabrics of all manners of colours and patterns, and all other accoutrements were required. So having so many jobs, the Porcupine could not call the older Lady at all, for were it to start, there would undoubtedly be no end until he had gently passed away with age and a horse's voice, which are deep and harsh, and she had become a far older, older Lady, though this would have only made her far more, more adorable. So instead the Porcupine busied itself, preparing all the necessities and accoutrements, hoping the older Lady would not wander off, as she tended to do and forget to come knitting by the fire, though she never did, wishing it had just a slightly simpler job so that it could call the older Lady without needing to be hoping and wishing so terribly much.

To this end, the Porcupine tried many things. First, he wrapped his tail in the yarn so that the yarn didn't snag and knot as yarn likes to do, especially those tiresome kinds of shaggy dog yarn, and the Porcupine called the older Lady.

'Dear older Lady, dear older Lady,
It's time my tail is yarned…' but the Porcupine realised that the older Lady may not believe it and cut short.

Next, the Porcupine looped the threads ready to be stitched and thought surely that this was an appropriate activity to call for and so began to.

'Dear older Lady, dear older Lady,
It's time for threads to loop…' but from then on the Porcupine could not think of any word to rhyme with loop other than cheeky words, for the Porcupine had two cheeks so tended to occasionally be slightly cheeky. Now it is unclear exactly what cheeky words filled the Porcupine's mind for no one has yet uninvented time, so we can hardly go back to ask, and the Porcupine surely wouldn't remember now. But instead of thinking poorly of the Porcupine now, as old thoughts are difficult to remember for which if you need proof, you only need to look at the Squirrel who can't find a single nut that it had previously buried, we should simply hazard a guess. For my part, I imagine the Porcupine was thinking of the French West-Indian island of Guadeloupe. Either way, since all calls had to rhyme, the Porcupine gave up.

Last, and quite a lot the least successful, the Porcupine turned its cheeky attention to the needles. The Porcupine, from experience of watching the older Lady prick her fingers on the needles, knew that sometimes the older Lady pricked her fingers on the needles. The trouble, at least it seemed so to the Porcupine, was that kept in the clackety metal tin that they were, it was hard for the older Lady to remove one needle by its long shaft without pricking a finger on

another needle's tapered sharp end. If only all needles were securely held with their duller ends on display and sharper ends concealed, what if, thought the Porcupine, it held the needles as such. However, with only four stubby legs, each, without exception, lacking any sign of fingers and only one bushy tail, for it was a Bush-tailed Porcupine, it could not hold the needles, dull end or sharp. Then, in less of a stroke and more of a hurtle of genius, the Porcupine thought to stick the needles into its back. If the needles were in the Porcupine's soft-like-a-cotton-pad back, then the sharp ends of the needles would be, as it were, padded. However, with only four stubby legs and each with the aforementioned lack of any sign of fingers, the Porcupine could not reach its back to place anything in, let alone a needle. So the Porcupine had another hurtle of genius, for, as we all know, hurtles of anything never come one at a time. If the Porcupine ate the needles and pushed them out its back from the inside, it would end to the same effect. The Porcupine often ate tree bark and conifer needles in the cold months, which would later be referred to as winter, so eating knitting needles wouldn't be all too different.

The Porcupine dipped its head ready to eat the needles from the dull end first, for that's the end that would have to be pushed out its back first for the older Lady to take, and there's no reason why proper manners of first in, first out wouldn't be observed here. Just before its little tongue wrapped itself around the needles, pursed lips, it spoke.

It has been pointed out before that at this point in the story, it was confusing as to whether the Porcupine spoke, or the needle spoke. Considering the needle has no mouth, lungs, tongue, vocal cords, or, as far as anyone can tell, the desire to say anything, the thought that the needle spoke would seem quite preposterous. But those who are preposterous are simply before the poster, and those who are only poster are surely after the er, which leaves everyone just er, thinking I suppose, which is exactly what the Porcupine did for a moment.

This had never happened to a needle before, and so in a state of shock, the Porcupine left its little tongue out and lips pursed for the whole of the conversation. And this is what it said,

'You shan't fool me,' the Porcupine said with a splutter. 'I'm sharp as a steel trap. Were I to eat the dull end first, I would be full of dull moments. So look sharp! I'll eat the other end first. Besides, I'm often told I have a cheeky, sharp tongue, so I'm sure I can handle it,' and with that and no other thought, the Porcupine ate the needles, sharp end first and pushed them out its back, with, indeed, no dull moments.

The Porcupine then called the older Lady, now with a simpler job with which to call.

'Dear older Lady, dear older Lady,
It's time to sit and sew.
Dear older Lady, my dear, made plain or lacy,
From me, needles now grow,' but as the older Lady sat down in her cosy armchair in the sitting room to sew, she reached for a needle from the Porcupine's back and, quite unrelaxingly, was pricked most terribly.

'Oh, you horrid little thing,' said the cat.

'Oh, you horrid little thing,' said the dog, having not heard the cat moments before, therefore making a mistake that would be a source of amusement for the two for at least three years to come, until the cat loses favour with the dog, and they begin to quarrel. 'You've pricked our dear older lady. Had you eaten the dull ends first it would have been okay, but now you are all spiny, and no animal should have any spines other than the one in their back.' And with this, they sent the Porcupine from the house to never take care of an older Lady again, especially not theirs, for she was quite a bit older, which made her that much more adorable.

WHY THE WHALE BLEW OUT ITS BLOWHOLE

If you now ask your father, though austere he might be, why the Whale has a blowhole, I imagine he will gladly and confidently answer that that said blowhole is in order to breathe. He will then quite possibly go on to explain that the Whale is a mammal just like you and I and your father too, and we all need to breathe air. Your father though, unwittingly, is entirely correct and entirely in. Indeed, we, as the Whale, need to breathe air, but this has as little to do with why the Whale has its blowhole as why the Elephant has a long nose. The issue lies in the fact that your father, who is wise by percentage as he is old by years, is not yet one hundred, and I fear that even if he were, he would need to be older to have heard of this story. So, assuming your father gives his blessing, I will endeavour to clarify why the Whale has its blowhole and what the Whale did to get it, just so, in truth.

In the best and worst of times, the age of wisdom and foolishness, the summer of camisoles and autumn of caftans, and madness of men and animals both, there was the vast division of land and ocean. The grand tempestuous ocean, deep with sunken valleys and coral forests, in many ways contrasted and in others complimented the furiously rugged land, towered by mountains and pine forests, and all animals, great and small, chose one within which to live. All animals bar one, the Whale.

The Whale, now submerged in the ocean but breathing the air of the land, was once the only animal to whom a side did not belong, for it wouldn't choose one. The Whale loved nothing more than a swim in the ocean currents, followed by a bask in the sun on the soft grass plain, as grass was softer then, for it was counted in quills rather than blades. But those quills of grass were being trampled, and the ocean waters were being muddied in the First World Dispute.

The animals of the ocean felt their sunken valleys greater than the towering mountains of the land, which didn't sit well with the animals of the land. And the animals of the land felt their pine forests more impressive than the coral forests of the ocean, whilst the animals of the ocean resoundingly disagreed. And to this effect, everything began to get a little foul, especially the play.

The Crab and the Lobster scuttled onto the land and snipped the heads off each yellow buttercup, so the land animals had to make do with glasses of margarine, which couldn't be believed to be butter. This also meant that in the years to come, when the animals would play a game not yet invented but known sociably as Hogwash, they would not be able to have a team all spread with yellow butter and would have to make do with yellow buttons instead. Anyway, since the game hadn't yet been discovered, this didn't concern the land animals much, though it is ironic that it was the Squirrel who took the

most offence. So in retaliation, though possibly before, the Squirrel and the Chipmunk scurried into the ocean and nibbled through the seaweed, leaving only seagrass for the ocean animals to smoke their cheese over, which despite being the same thing didn't feel like it and was not what they wanted.

The Dogfish chased the Cat up a tree and left it there, unable to climb down, for it is apparent that cat legs don't work that way. Though now that you've brought it up in my words, it might simply be that cats, like the smoke from smoked cheese, like to go and remain upwards, and that in turn once reaching the top of a tree, unlike any kind of smoke I am familiar with, like to sing about it when they get there. Either way, the Dog chased the Catfish down into a hole and left it there, unable to swim back up, for I suppose catfish fins don't work that way either.

The Crocodile and the Alligator crept ashore and lay on rocks, taking in all the sunlight, for they too are cold blooded but usually get their heat from underwater hotspots, which also give great reception so everyone feels welcome and left no sunlight for the Iguana or the Lizard. The Iguana and the Lizard slipped afloat and lay on reefs, drinking up all the ocean water, for they too drink water but usually get their water from springs, though for tea they use hot springs and left no water for the Crocodile or the Alligator. Though in both cases, it seemed that all four animals were simply cutting off their noses to spite their faces, for neither the Crocodile nor the Alligator was cold and neither the Iguana nor the Lizard thirsty, explaining why all four have no discernible noses anymore and make do with pin-holes.

And the Whale was between all this madness, and considering that the Whale was so large, it was unusual for it to be between anything. So one day, the Whale called an assembly on the sands. The ocean animals lined along the coast with the tips of their flippers in the wet sand, and the land animals lined facing them with the tips of their toes in the dry sand, with the Whale standing between them all. Mayhem to its left, and mayhem to its right, all squallered and blundered.

'Be quiet, will you!' bellowed the Whale, and all animals fell still, except the little Mouse who squeaked once more and felt terribly embarrassed for it. 'I've tried reason, but you shall not hear it.'

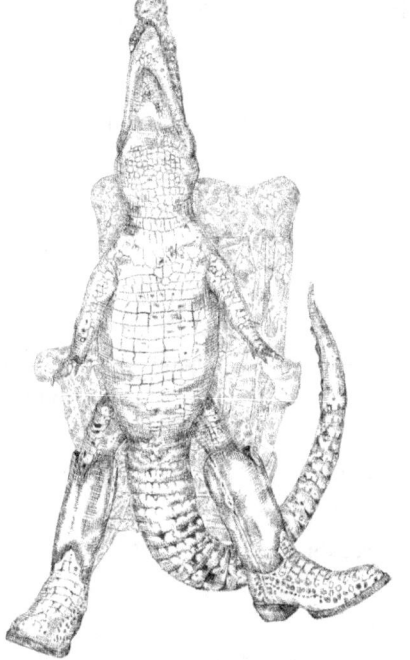

Why the whale blew out its blowhole **53**

'Hear, hear!' called the Man and Monkey in unison, who then proceeded with some snickering together, before the Monkey fell from the tree, thump on top of the Man's head.

'So I propose a competition, or game, if you will. Which shall be judged by the old Limpets, for they live on the rocky shore between ocean and land. We shall call it', and the Whale thought for a moment, first the name 'Hogwash' came to mind, but since the Whale minded the name too much, it simply wouldn't do, 'the old Limpet's games! And the winner shall be right.'

'We shall show you crusty land animals whose rock formations are the most striking,' called the Oyster, the Pipefish, and the Squid.

'Nay,' replied the Antelope, the Red Fox, and the Man to the Horses disbelief, 'you salty ocean animals. It is we who,' the fox looked at the Man. 'Whom?'

'Whome,' replied the Man, though pronouncing the 'e' silently. 'Wome,' chirped the Cricket.

'Womomomonum,' blubbered the Sea-elephant, and the mayhem started anew.

'Be quiet, will you!' bellowed the Whale again, and all animals fell still, especially the little Mouse, who covered its little mouth tightly with both its little paws. 'Old Limpets, what shall the first old Limpet's game be?' asked the Whale, though, in truth, all animals wished to know. The Limpets conferred for a moment and finally answered.

'A whistling competition!' With which a raucous of cries broke out, for this new event was far more interesting than any had anticipated, and they couldn't continue until they had gathered and put all the cries away again. So eventually the Whale opened the games and ceremoniously tossed a beach shell into the air, and all the animals' heads arched back, and eyes rolled following the shell as it floated down. 'Dry side-up,' announced the Whale. 'The game shall be held on the land.' Cheers and jeers and general commotion restarted with gusto.

Since it was to be held on land, it was decided the ocean animals would go first. The Oyster began. Having observed the sun and sky through the water, the Oyster had a clear understanding of land air, so opened its shell to whistle, but without being able to feel the air rush in as it might in the water, and without any lips, no sound it made, and the Oyster sunk ashamedly deep into the wet sand.

Next, the Pipefish was to go, and with the name it had, it was very confident indeed. The Pipefish opened its long mouth and breathed in with its long chest, right down to its longest fin and let out the longest stream of bubbles any animal had ever seen. Each bubble drifted up, hovered for a moment and made a tremendous pop, which sent all the ocean animals into roarous huzzahs. However, after much deliberation, the old Limpets ruled that to burst a bubble and to blow the whistle were two distinctly separate things, despite having similar imagery.

So finally the Squid was up, whom it was all down to. The Squid spread its eight arms and two tentacles, which should never be confused, and crouched head down. Each of the eight tentacles and two arms quivered from its nib, a quiver that shuddered and ran down each limb in a shot and let out a fountain of black ink that rained down on the ocean animals, followed by a faint, high-pitched peep. The land animals burst into laughter, tumbling and rolling around in the dry sand.

Quite confident that they would win and end this dispute for once and always, the Antelope stood up majestically. The Antelope, never making a sound from its mouth, decided rather controversially to whistle with its hooves by leaping from place to place and making a clip and a clap, irrespective of whether this would have been accepted by the old Limpets or not, being on dry sand, not even the feeblest paperclip was heard.

So then the Red Fox stepped up, still quite confident, but accidentally dipped its forelegs in the squid's ink and ruined the beautifully unstripped pelt it had had since being a kit. The Panda chuckled a little, which it regretted a lot as the Red Fox walloped it, giving it a black eye, and entirely flustered, the Red Fox wrapped its paws in foxgloves and skulked away.

So finally it was the Man's turn. The Man was known, at least in some parts by some people, though mostly locally by a few supportive friends, for its tuneful whistle. Not quite as melodic as a bird's but nonetheless better than a squid's peep.

But having been thumped on the head by the fallen Monkey, it had bitten its tongue and made no more than a rasping splutter. And as it did so, blew a juicy raspberry, which had snuck into its mouth earlier, clean across the beach and hit the old Limpets, who deducted points for absurdity.

It seemed that then the competition was over with no clear triumphant winner, though both sides energetically appealed to the old Limpets.

'Be quiet, will you!' bellowed the Whale, and all animals fell still for the final time, the little Mouse having now buried its little head in the sand, something the Ostrich saw and took note of. 'I shall get a try,' and the Whale took such a deep breath that all the animals' fins, tails, feathers, manes, and other extremities fluttered towards the Whale's huge mouth, which, as it closed, made them all drop to the sandy floor still pointing in the Whale's direction. The Whale began to blow, but it couldn't purse its huge lips, so no air came out at all. The Whale blew harder and harder, but without pursed lips, no air was coming out. Such a huge amount of air being pushed by such force must go somewhere, thought all the animal spectators as they took a step back, and sure enough, it did. The air burst out of the Whale's back, creating a huge plume of water through a blowhole, and a cloud of clear smoke, like one hundred teapots on the hob, accompanied by the blast of a loud long and sharp whistle, like one hundred teapots on the hob.

With the ears of all the animals of the ocean and all the animals of the land still ringing, the old Limpets proclaimed the Whale as the winner of the first old Limpet's games. The Whale then gladly proclaimed the grand ocean's deep sunken valleys to be equally striking as the rugged land's towering mountains, the coral forests as beautiful as the pine forests, and the mayhem to be done with. 'For', said the Whale, 'I won these games, and therefore I am right. So when in the future your pups and kits and fry ask who was right, tell them it was I, and call me the Whale.'

WHY THE SHEEP ATE A CLOUD

Many things in this world are similar to other things in this world. A zebra crossing is similar to a notebook, which is similar in turn to a book collection carefully standing between two wooden elephants on a shelf, because they are all lined. A street is similar to a Shepherd's pie or most savoury foods because they are all, despite what you might think, better off without jams. However, nothing is quite like the Sheep. So if you were wondering what was like the Sheep, you should know, it's nothing. But surely something must be like the Sheep? If you ask your parents, they might say that cotton-wool is like the Sheep, though that would be a little silly of them to say, or they might tell you that a cloud is like a Sheep. The cloud analogy is a close one, but if you really think about it, they are not alike, as a cloud is found in the sky, and a Sheep is not. But all this analogy may have, and probably did, in fact quite definitely so, befall the Sheep because it ate a cloud. Now there is no good story that starts by revealing the ending, so let us hope that this story is that much better than good, as, if you indulge me, I will tell you why the Sheep ate a cloud, just so, in truth.

It is now reasonably well-known that a strawberry frosted with sugar powder makes an adorably gratifying afternoon sweet, whereas a pebble sprinkled with golden sand makes something horribly unappetising, and yet few have eaten a pebble sprinkled with golden sand. This is all possible and simply explained because of the Ample Taste, where all living things and some dozy slumbering things all acquired their taste for this or that. The events of this story sprung up near the end of the Ample Taste, when nearly all things had been tried and tested, and some were found wanting garnish, when the Pigeon learnt its preference for crumbs over cactuses...

and the Mouse, its preference for Cheese over Charcoal or even cheese smoked over charcoal but not the charcoal itself.

So here where tastes were being exhausted, claimed by their consumers, the skinny, for it had a lot of skin and little else, Sheep, settled on grass. Grass was not the juiciest of tastes, though it could be juicy, nor was it the most exotic, or exotic at all really, but the Sheep had its reasons for preferring grass over gooseberries, other than gooseberries already having been claimed by the Goose for name's sake. Grass, you see, could be found almost anywhere, and the Sheep liked to eat, almost anywhere.

Sometimes the Wolf, who had chosen a preference for bacon over brick, took refuge from its pursuit of three sizzlingly delicious looking pieces of bacon, as they took to hiding inside houses of brick, which the Wolf couldn't stomach at all, and dressed up as the Sheep. This, note, was not because the Wolf liked the feeling of being a sheep or being sheepish at all – in fact, this was quite opposed to the Wolf's nature. The Wolf dressed up partly because it made a nice change but also to sneakily eat the Sheep's grass without being caught out. Besides, it was easy enough to dress in the Sheep's clothing if the wolf shaved and put a bow and jumper on as the Sheep did, for the Sheep was praised for the best fence jumper around.

The Sheep, however, knew that the Wolf would do this from time to time, partly because the Boy would run around town shouting so, and partly because once in a while the Boy was right. The Sheep thought and pondered and mused until it inspired an idea in itself – to make a mark. That being said, the Sheep surely wanted to make a mark on the world, but first decided to make a mark on itself. Had it a mark, the Sheep mused, the Wolf could not masquerade as itself and eat all of its grass. So the Sheep went and got the best marker pen that it could find and gave itself a beauty spot. The beauty spot it gave was indeed in the most beautiful spot any animal had ever seen, depicting the famous scene from the story of the last Sheep, where they celebrated turning wine into water and bread into grass or something. However, the Wolf did not find itself wanting, that is the Wolf's self, to have such a scene permanently marked on its back, just as the Sheep had suspected it mightn't. But instead, the Wolf rubbed a spot of mud on its back, which was hardly of equal quality but was otherwise exactly the same, except for where it differed, which the Wolf corrected with a biro.

So then the Sheep mused further and finally decided to get an ornament much like a bangle in that it was showy, but much unlike a bangle as it was not cheap. This ornament not entirely unlike a bangle was worn like a bracelet and had lined across it a line of charms. There were three charms the shapes of pigs behind one the shape of a brick, and one the shape of a bonnet and shawl much like a hood and one the shape of Romulus stroking the Eagle, and one the shape of sugar-free peppermint chewing gum, but all shapes of things the Wolf could not stand. It is important to note on the Wolf's behalf that it didn't like the peppermint chewing gum because it was prone to huffing and puffing, so pepper tickled its nose and disagreed with the Wolf entirely. That being said, the Wolf, not being able to stand these things, was unable to look like the sheep at all, just as the Sheep had suspected it mightn't, and for all the Sheep's musing, the Wolf had gotten entirely bemused. Though after much effort with good words and compliments, the Wolf made other charms hardly of equal quality but otherwise exactly the same, except for where they differed, which the Wolf corrected by shaping spearmint, for it suited the Wolf's teeth, sugar-full chewing gum into the desired shapes.

The Sheep, thinking it had no choice but to eat something of which the Wolf would always be pilfering from, reassured then that it too would have to vary its diet, or it may come across a patch of grass where the grass had already been munched on and was then unable to eat almost anywhere. The Sheep thought deeply about it for a moment, or to be precise, the amount of time it takes to chew the cud, and concluded that the best new food to try was wriggling insect. The Sheep had an origami, being that of many-fold, of reasons for this. First, wriggling insect was a food group not yet chosen by any other animal in the neighbourhood, though the Birds were considering it, but then they did prefer seeds to almost everything else, especially socks, which they didn't like at all.

Secondly, if the Sheep was to sneak a taste of wriggling insect now and then, it would be when it had nothing else, such as grass, to eat, which was surprisingly convenient as wriggling insect often appeared in patches of soil that regrettably lacked grass. Thirdly, and the final reason that is worth mentioning presently, wriggling insect is often pink in colour, whereas grass is green or yellow-green, depending on if you're on this side or the other. So the Sheep went to find the wriggling insect that might become its wriggling insect dish, but there were none to be found. It, you see, hadn't rained in a long time, and as the pitter patter of rain hadn't knocked on the ground to bring the wriggling insect to its front door to see who was calling, it was all as snug as, well, a bug, under the ground.

The Sheep, being a smart little number, maybe eight, knew that for there to be rain, there must be clouds. Now, clouds were quite mysterious things, floating high up in the sky, and the Sheep had never heard how they were made, but it supposed, and this is what it supposed – the clouds are made when people discard a white marshmallow because they prefer pink marshmallows to polyester mittens, mostly because the former isn't as itchy as the latter. So the white marshmallows get sad and light headed and, despite being downcast, float upwards like a balloon. So the Sheep made its way to the news agency that had just opened in order to stock all of the new delicacies and tastes being acquired and to occasionally give news about who or what acquired them.

'Welcome customer. Come in, come in. What's your taste?' beckoned the incredibly gruntled clerk, no doubt because business was going so well. 'Will you be having loganberries, I'm sure you'll prefer them to light bulbs, though we also stock the bulbs.'

'No, no. Thank you.'

'Well, then how about a thistle, thorny but far preferable to a thimble?' The Sheep suspected as much because it sometimes accidentally would eat a thistle with its grass and rather liked them, whereas a thimble, it had never tried. But since you shouldn't knock something until you try it, which is why doorbells were invented as very few wanted actually to eat a door, the Sheep couldn't say for certain.

'No, no. One sweetie bag, please.'

'Ah yes, ah yes,' the Clerk said, fumbling around in one drawer then moving to another before returning to the first and back to the Sheep.

'There you are, one sweet tea-bag,' the Clerk announced.

'No, no. Sorry. A sweetie bag. A bag of sweets,' repeated the Sheep. 'Ah yes, we have liquorice Bonbons or Butterscotch Humbugs, and we have any sweet you could eat. What's your taste?' asked the Clerk, hovering, with its hands over several drawers, in anticipation.

'I'd just like a bag of marshmallows, please. All white.'

'Ah yes, that's ok. Here you go.' With which the Clerk put a bag of

pink marshmallows on the table.

'Sorry, I said all white.'

'Ah yes, that's ok. But pardon, what did you say?'

'Not pink, all white.'

'All right, all right, but what colour would you like?'

'All white, as in all of them in the colour white, the white colour.'

'Ah yes,' said the Clerk fumbling around in the back. 'One bag of all white, all right marshmallows. That'll be two shillings, please,' said the Clerk. But since money was a new-fangled thing, many were still wary of it, and the Sheep had none.

'I'm afraid I have none,' said the Sheep, looking ever so afraid and a little sorry.

'Would this box of staples do?'

'Ah yes, that'll do nicely,' said the Clerk while wrapping the marshmallows and quite absent-mindedly the staples too, in newspaper clippings and masking tape.

Thanking the Clerk politely, the Sheep left the news agency and then, as one does just as it's too late to do anything about it, realised its error. If it bought a bag of all white, all right marshmallows, in order to use the white ones, it couldn't then discard them, and in turn, they wouldn't get light headed and float up to become clouds. So the Sheep thought, pondered, and mused one last time, opened the bag, and started shouting. This is what the Sheep shouted,

'You white marshmallows you.' The Sheep wasn't accustomed to shouting profanities, so this was the best it could do. 'You, you are disgusting. Well, not disgusting, but I prefer watermelons to white marshmallows. So, yeah,' and as the Sheep shouted this, the little white marshmallows were so disheartened they became all faint and light-headed, as they have such a sensitive temperament, and began to float upwards. 'Yeah, you. I wouldn't eat you unless I were peckish, and it was too early for dinner,' shouted the sheep, though immediately regretting it. Clearly the Sheep had gone too far, and unlike when walking in the grass in slippers but realising that the slippers had slipped off, as they are annoyingly named for doing, there was no going back to fetch them, and the white marshmallows began to cry. Presently, they were over a thick grassy patch and rain here wouldn't tipper tap on the ground enough to call the wriggling insect to the surface, but the Sheep couldn't stop them and had no way of containing them either.

'Hush now. There there. I'm sorry. Look,' said the Sheep, taking one of the white marshmallows and eating it up. 'Mmm, delicious,' said the Sheep, rubbing its naked stomach satisfied, but although this was, of course, an act, it was also quite true, so the Sheep ate another and another.

Now the expression 'you are what you eat' is clearly absurd as, if we were what we ate, we'd all be cannibals, and a lot more of us would be varieties of sandwiches, but in this case, the expression seems more suitable. With its head in the clouds, the Sheep gobbled up every last white marshmallow, which filled its body and then some, until the Sheep literally, and not in the ironically witless use of the word, became a puffy marshmallow cloud. This in the end though sufficed well enough, as the Wolf could no longer disguise itself as the Sheep so well, and the look kind of flattered the Sheep.

WHY THE MOLE LOST ITS EYES

If you have ever seen your own face, you, no doubt, marked there were two eyes, one nose between them, and one mouth below that. But imagine what big and little people alike thought hundreds of years ago, when there were no mirrors or means of seeing their own faces. It wouldn't be too unreasonable to assume that they often panicked on whether they had the correct number of eyes and noses and mouths, and whether they were in the correct locations on their faces. Such a line of thought I both admire and encourage and might lead you to think upon the Mole. The Mole, who by now lives mostly underground, and who has, as far as it seems, no eyes. If this thought occurs to you, I suggest doing two things quite immediately – examine a mirror to confirm the number and location of parts on your face, just in case, and question your parents on why the Mole has no eyes. However, despite having two ears on the sides of their heads, parents often can't seem to connect them to the words that come out of their mouths and might respond with something along the lines of Moles having small eyes but not needing to see much in the dark or, in other words, gibberish. So, if this has all occurred in much the same order as I have supposed, and left you wondering and on the verge of a panic, check the mirror once more, just to be sure, and then lend me your ears, just for a moment or three so that I can explain why the Mole has no eyes, just so, in truth.

In the last days of March, before it had gone to the hairdresser's so madness was quite set in, all sorts of grounded fops and bookish fools queued in circles around the garden's bucket drawn water well – in triangles around the hammock that swung from three trees, and in all manners of polygons, polyhedra, and polytopes that contorted those queuing into uniquely fashionable positions. They queued in all shapes, in fact, other than a straight line, for each participant in the queue, only seeing one slightly less disgruntled participant before them, had no inkling in what direction the queue should naturally proceed and so most hazarded a usually terribly mistaken guess. They all wound around the small coffee-shop, in which worked the gifted, though down only to hard work and practice, fine creative called the Craftsy Mole, and it almost deserved it. For they were all there to watch the fine creations the Craftsy Mole could produce, and if the wallet allowed it, to purchase one of the finished eggs. The Craftsy Mole was the finest and most creative egg designer in all of March and was predicted to continue to be at least so until the dog days when all canines carve and sell their plaques so that the focus is taken a little from the moler's work, though it didn't mind the rest. Now, what the significance of this story occurring in March is, and how the dogs received their name that lends itself so well to dental puns are both good questions to ask, something I am often encouraging you to do. Suffice to say that at this point, the Mole did not lose its eyes per se – the Mole knows where they are, it just can't find them. But I jump ahead of myself.

The Craftsy Mole had not always been a creative. Its father was in constructions and helped dig and lay the foundations of new build-ings, such as great libraries and museums. Hoping his child would follow in his paw prints, Father Mole often took Baby Mole, as at the time the Craftsy Mole was only a baby and thusly known, to work to learn the tricks of the trade. There were, in fact, many tricks to learn, such as neither to dig at the same time with both hands nor to only

dig with one, for you would end up digging back around to yourself rather than straight down, but to alternate. This may seem obvious to you and me, as though we may not be in constructions, and we have all been to the beach or sandy areas or pestered our parents digging for information, but none of this seems so obvious to a baby who can not yet ask questions.

Digging was fine for the Baby Mole, but just fine, and nothing that is just fine can make anyone more than just content, therefore, digging was simply contentious, which the Baby Mole found rather quarrelsome. However, at Father Mole's work one Spring, much like the time our story takes place in the present, though not the current present, the Toddler Mole, for it had grown an inch or so, mischievously and utterly unpermittedly entered one of the great libraries that also had a lot of artefacts or museums that stocked piles of books, no one was really sure. Toddler Mole shuffled around looking through books, boxes, board games, and heirlooms of bygone times when it came across a small door, behind which was a small back room completely out of sight unless one went to the back of the building. In the middle of this room was a pedastool, which was either undoubtedly a stool for feet or a stool for children, and since the Toddler Mole was a child with feet, which it checked to make sure, the stool was clearly in some way or other for itself. Upon the pedastool sat a glass frame blown into a detailed birdcage oval, and in this glass frame perched an egg. The egg shone golden and black, sheened precious stones bed in precious metals, and shimmered stories of love and revenge and the gigantic Teumessian Fox of Greek mythology, or possibly a raccoon; either way, the Toddler Mole thought to itself how nifty a thing the egg was and from then on could think of little else.

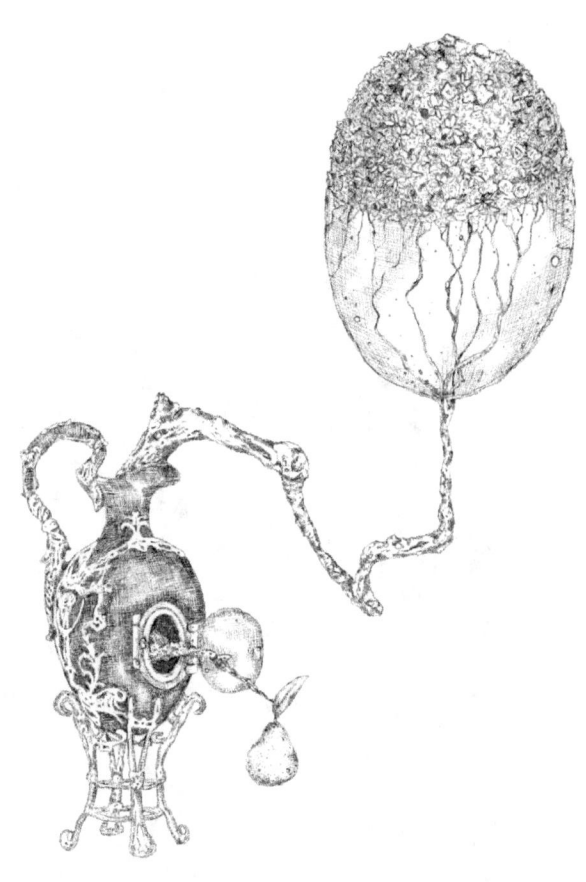

Eventually growing another inch or so, it was time for the Mole, who with its size but by lack of distinguishing skills yet was simply known so, had to leave its father and make its way in the wide and deep world, for being from a digging family, the Mole was acutely aware of at least those two dimensions the world had plenty of.

The Mole began by taking a part-time job at a boules green, where it had to find and remove worms and other grubs from the lawn for their own safety. The Mole got very good at this, though the Worms showed little to no appreciation for it, assuming that rolling into a ball was not worm-talk for 'many thanks, you young wipper-snapper, most kind!' though usually it just seemed like rolling into a ball. However, in the evenings, the Mole would paint the boules in golds and blacks and then colours of its own devising. The Mole began to get so apt at this that it became known to the other staff or late night visitors to the green as the Crafty Mole, for all his night sneakings.

After the Mole felt it had learnt all it could there, it was time to move horizontally onwards until it came to a hill, which it moved upwards, where it found a small coffee-shop with a bucket drawn water well and swinging hammock tied across two trees. Entering for a respite and small cup of black coffee, the Crafty Mole got into an incredibly fruitful conversation with the coffee-shop Proprietor. They spoke of gooseberries and grapes, of apples and pears, but the Crafty Mole said that it preferred eggs to them all. Hearing the whole of the story to this point, the Proprietor offered the Crafty Mole a job right there on the spot. This made conversation a little strained as the spot was just slightly too far from where the Mole sat to allow for a comfortable conversation and so both had to raise their voices a little.

'I use an egg in each cup of coffee I make,' said the Proprietor. Sensing the Crafty Mole wonder, the comment did not go unexplained, 'I believe to make an eggcellent cup of coffee, it is necessary, as that is where the word comes from after all.' Hesitating for a minute but not wanting to be a stickler for pronunciation and staying true to his name, the Crafty Mole let it pass.

'But now I am left with hundreds of empty egg shells I carefully drilled, blew, and drained, and nowhere to put them. What's more, some regretfully crack, but I don't want them to feel any less of an egg, so still use them for my coffee.'

'Why not use them in an omelette?' asked the Crafty Mole.

'The cracks are unintentional, you see,' explained the Proprietor. 'So won't you stay and make my egg shells into something more eggstraordinary?'

'Indeed, I would be eggcited to do so,' replied the Crafty Mole with a playful smirk that was surely lost on the Proprietor. 'Though I suggest making your coffee with only the cream of the crop, I'm sure no other coffee shop would or could make such increamable coffee,' the Mole suggested, now having a whale of a time, especially as it was still wailing across the room. 'Then the eggs could, in fact, be made into small omelettes or the like, with a little salt.'

The Proprietor thought this a wonderful idea and renamed the coffee shop the Eggsalted Hilltop Coffee Shop and decided to rename the Crafty Mole while at it. The Proprietor renamed the Crafty Mole to the Craftsiest Mole, but when the Mole pointed out that there was one too many s's, the Proprietor dropped the latter and changed it to the Craftsy Mole, who decided to let it be, which brings us to the current times, though not the present current but the current of the story.

Through the whispers of the trees who had no use for eggs, decorative or otherwise, but who liked to house them in their branches nonetheless, the news of the Craftsy Mole spread. Animals came from all around the hilltop, and as each finally was able to enter the Eggsalted Hilltop Coffee Shop, they were met with wonder. The smells of the creamy coffee, the tastes of the light salted omelettes, and the spectacle of hundreds of dozens of intricately painted, much like Ukrainian Easter eggs but richer looking, with gold cuffs and hinges that open to reveal a small soft silk cushion inside, or sometimes an intricately painted inner lining like the stained glass windows of the great Churches the Craftsy Mole would also visit with its father as a baby, egg shells. Needless to say that the focus of their wonderment and of our story is the eggs, so I'll simply add briefly here that they had devised an ingenious way to light salt the omelettes that involved sea-water and a large light bulb. The eggs varied in shape, some being more oval and others more spherical, and varied in size, some being bigger and others being smaller, but each had a uniquely mesmerising design so that were any child to look upon any one, it would be no wonder the rapture they felt and the dedication they might make of a lifetime to the art.

So at the time, as April was setting in, five particularly foppish and fool-hearty patrons entered in what could be described as a goggle, though only one was a goose. In order, they came, and in order, they spoke. The first being the Ostrich, 'What lovely eggs,' it guffawed, as Ostriches do. 'I have brought one of my own. Won't you please paint and design it?' This was the first time the Craftsy Mole had been commissioned, so three things occurred almost simultaneously to it – that this was the first time it had been commissioned, which was exciting, that Ostrich eggs are the biggest and strongest of all birds, which was easier, and that Ostrich legs were awfully powerful. The third not being of much relevance other than the Craftsy Mole not wanting the Ostrich to kick over and crack all of its work either in disappointment or eggcitement and so replied, 'I'll do the best I can.' Which it certainly did and without the use of any eyeglasses. When finally the Ostrich egg was done, it was magnificent, with a deep maroon and matte black stitched pattern of the night sky and golden constellations that truly appeared to twinkle like little stars. As a final touch, it was placed on a golden three-legged stand of Victorian elaborate floral design, with an eclectic mix of fittings and ending in three gorgeous gold artichoke feet.

'That is truly astonishing,' the Goose, who entered with the Ostrich but second, honked nasally, 'I have brought one of my own also. Won't you please paint and design it?' Having accepted the Ostrich's request, the Craftsy Mole couldn't eggxactly refuse, besides it was still flattered, and the Goose was known for being temperamental, Motherly, and story-telling this day and then laying golden eggs that, and indeed the egg the Goose presented was of the pure golden kind, as clearly the Goose had eaten a lot of carrots. So the Craftsy Mole decided to, instead of painting over the naturally lavish colouring, put on its eyeglasses and start carving a precisely elaborate scene. It unfolded before the onlookers as a fabulous etching of a woodpecker in an apple tree, with each feather hair and leaf vein glistening in the freshly whittled gold.

'Astounding. Simply Astounding,' quacked the duck, as it had always been told it quacked like a duck and didn't like to disappoint, who entered with the other two but third. 'I have brought one of my own too. Won't you please paint and design it?' The Craftsy Mole accepted without hesitation, as the eggs it usually painted and designed from the salted omelettes were of the salted duck variety, though despite the name, sometimes oriental hen eggs. So the Craftsy Mole turned down the next lens of its eyeglasses, as it couldn't very well give anything less complexly effortful to the Duck as it had to the other two. After one painstaking hour and six bittersweet minutes, it was revealed. It, with thin webbing thread around dividing scenes of epic Aegean poems, bid unwritten stories in earthy powdered inks of crushed shells and florets, stories that narrated adventures so monumental it seemed an epic illusion they could all be told on the back of an eggshell.

'Slap me flabbergast. Your eggscapes are simply lyrical,' the Hummingbird chimed, who entered with the three so far but stepped forth. 'I have brought one of my own to add. Won't you please paint and design it?' Now, this was a true shock to the Craftsy Mole, who had never imagined painting or designing what it believed to be the smallest egg lain anywhere or at least anywhere around the hilltop. This being the challenge of a lifetime, the Hummingbird could not be refused. Turning its eyeglasses to the strongest magnification they could muster and squinching its eyes somewhat, its work was of such minitude that even the onlookers present couldn't see it until the Craftsy Mole stepped back and prompted them to lean in. With the tiniest cut stencils and spray paint from rolled blades of St. Augustine grass of the Craftsy Mole's devision, it portrayed the world as it was then. The slumbering sea with its rolling waves on broken shores of sunbathed sands or rounded pebbles stumbled into reaching rivers, necks stretched up the hills and mountains to snow-capped peaks, and as each onlooker focussed harder, the milieu focussed in so that more and more was revealed.

'I can't bear to look away. It's just bewitching,' lathered the Salmon, who entered with the other four but last. 'I have brought one of my own in like manner. Won't you please paint and design it?' The Craftsy Mole, not knowing if it were even possible, did not pause to even scrunch the top of its nose. Thinking back to the great library that also had a lot of artefacts or museum that stocked piles of books, no one was really sure, it wanted nothing more than to create a piece as glorious as the one that sat in the small back room. So with every shard of glass it could find attached to its eyeglasses, and with eyes so screwed, they appeared closed or simply appeared disappeared up until, with a 'pop', they did disappear.

The Craftsy Mole, unable to see at all, was distraught. Had it still had the use of its eyes, the Craftsy Mole would have been able to see in the reflections of all the shards of glass attached to its spectacles that its eyes were not now where they ought to be on its face but had entirely migrated. The Craftsy Mole stumbled out of the Eggsalted Hilltop Coffee Shop, stumbled past the crowds that by now had gotten themselves into such bizarre shapes I'm sure there is no name for them and, not knowing in what direction it was stumbling, went down. The Craftsy Mole dug and dug until it too disappeared under the soil and earth, leaving only a mound. In fact, it made the whole mountain, or, at least the hilltop, into a molehill. It dug as its father did and, without any eyes, never dug back. No one, at least to this tale's knowledge, has ever seen what the Craftsy Mole was painting on the salmon egg, or whether it was completed at all, though if it were, it would surely be the most exquisite treasure ever craftsed.

The Meerkat's riddle

The Meerkats were thinking about many things, but mostly ideas kept popping up with their heads, like, what happens if someone shouts loud enough for everyone to hear but is in a room of people who can't hear? At which point one Meerkat had taken it upon itself to invert and start shouting loud-enough-for-everyone-to-hear down their holes, causing more heads to pop up with more ideas.

'What happens when a bus that's always late arrives at a bus stop with a schedule behind what it ought to be?' asked one slightly less eloquent but insightful, or inciteful, Meerkat. 'Or at a bus stop with no schedule?' added another.

All these questions were keeping the Meerkats so preoccupied, being far too early to be occupied yet, that they didn't notice the Khan of those eastern plains approach, despite all its majesty.

On nearing the Meerkats, the Khan had found itself a little intrigued by all the ponderings, or possibly it had mistaken this kind of pondering for the like of frolicking around a pond, and seeking water had come by mishap, but being Khan no one would suggest such a thing. So it sat and observed for a while.

As the Khan watched, a few things became apparent – one of the few being that the Meerkats weren't so much addressing questions to anyone in particular but more simply saying what popped into their heads as their heads popped up. The other of the few things being that that was indeed the case right up until it wasn't, and one Meerkat looked it right in the eyes.

'Is this a ruse, sir?' it asked, but before the Khan could reply, another popped up having something clearly important to say. 'Speaking of roosters,' said the second, having quite possible misheard, 'what happens when a rooster that crows each morning lives in a country where the sun never sets?'

'Well, I…' the Khan stumbled and stuttered, 'it's,' luckily a noise much like mischief heading their way clearly popped all the Meerkats' ideas and invariably their heads also back into their holes. Leaving the Khan quite alone and taking a bite from a delicious looking dandelion, thinking about the Meerkat's puzzle.

WHY THE NIPPONJIKA WEARS VELVET CORAL ON ITS CROWN

If you thought that almost half of all animals had some kind of horn or antler on their heads, I fear you may be wrong, though it would be best to confirm with your mother anyway. However, such a thought is entirely reasonable, as many do. The Rhino, as it prefers to be known casually, took up its infamous horn a long while ago, though that's another story, and ever since then a lot of other animals have followed suit, some even before the Rhino. So all of this inevitably leads to the question, why does the Spotted Deer wear sticks on its head? Again, a very reasonable query, though I fear misguided. Those are in fact not sticks but, what most with a comparably sufficient grasp of English call, antlers. Though ask your mother, or anyone really, what an antler is, and they will certainly give no better explanation than them being sticks, and ask why the Spotted Deer wears them, and they will give no story better than what I could make up. However, this is no made up story. So if you truly want to learn why the Spotted Deer wears antlers on its head, take a seat, and let me tell you how the story developed, just so, in truth.

All fortuitous journeys are alike, in that they flourish with the arrival at the once determined destination, whereas each unfortuitous journey is unfortuitous in its own way. However, a journey is never as simple as that, so when multiple characters emerge – each with different perspectives on fortune, some feeling that it favours the bold, while others feeling it is made by every man who is an architect – whether the destination was arrived at and the journey fortuitous or not, is often in the eye of the beholder, which if not removed by a water solution should be consulted over with an optician.

This story, at least at first, begins with four unfortuitous journeys, each of which being a huge concern to, despite not having the faintest idea of it, the Nipponjika. The Nipponjika, also known as the Spotted Deer, for the obvious reasons that it had a soft speckling of creamy white spots across its back, and that it was a deer, lived on the eastern island of Nippon to which it owed its name and lived there quite happily at that. The Nipponjika, much like most other deer at this time, resembled a small horse with slender legs and wore nothing, especially no extraneous frills on its head, though now many do, having acquired them on various fortuitous journeys of their own and considering that the fashion really picked up in the early Curvusion period, a period often forgotten for all its eccentricities as it being so curved could not fit in a regular timeline. The Nipponjika, wise appropriate to its years, which were plentiful, was in many ways the Khan of the eastern plains. It did not hunt but ate only the four leaves of promising clovers and delicious yellow heads of dandelions, though left the lions teeth in tact for it needed them itself to eat.

While eating one such delicious yellow head, the Nipponjika was thinking over a puzzle posed to it by the nodding Meerkats when seemingly from nowhere, but actually from the Nipponjika's left, through the grassy shrubs came panting a little copy of itself, without spots. 'You have to help me,' it said to itself, panting. 'I'm being chased by the Farmer, the Elephant, the Crocodile, and the Hungry Tiger, all of whom would eat me, except the Elephant who would make do with stomping on my back.' All this sounded awfully hard on the little copy, and the Nipponjika could not bear to hear such a thing, especially from itself, despite it not having any spots.

'Here,' said the Nipponjika, 'I am in many ways the Khan of these eastern plains. If we cover my spots, they'll think you've grown into me and won't dare eat or stomp on, in the case of the Elephant, me.' This all along in fact being the little copy's cunning plan, for whether it stopped the four wanting to eat or stomp on, in the case of the Elephant, it or not, the results would be literally on the head of the Nipponjika and not itself, though they were practically the same. So they went to the marsh, whirring with dragonflies hunting skipping boatmen across the water, for a better view and rubbed dust and earth over the Nipponjika's spots until they had hidden away in its fur.

Now the Nipponjika and small trickster stood waiting with anticipation. However, the little copy found it hard to stand or sit still for long, as little things often do, and looked down at the marshy water in which it spotted a little dandesealion blocked by coral and velvety seaweed, which it had heard was extra-delicious and wanted immediately to try. It looked up at the Nipponjika tauntingly. 'If you are the Khan of these plains, where is your crown?'

'I do not need a crown,' replied the Nipponjika while still calmly scanning the distant bushes.

'Nonsense, every Khan needs a crown. How else will travellers know you are, in many ways, different from other deer? What if in fact the Farmer, the Elephant, the Crocodile, and the Hungry Tiger don't see you are the Khan and in fact eat or stomp on, in the case of the

Elephant, you? Look, there is some coral down in the marshy water, and if you scooped it up, you could wear it on your crown as the name dictates.' The Nipponjika thought it preposterous that any could not recognise it was the Khan, but as its little copy seemed so concerned, the Nipponjika thought it best to do as it asked if but to calm its little friend down. So it scooped its head down and pulled up the coral, which it then attached to its head.

Next, the little copy looked up and said, 'for sure you look the Khan now, but that coral is so rough and shelly, no one would believe you to be a great Khan of plains such as these. Why not reach down and wrap your new headwear in that velvet seaweed?' Again the little copy seemed at such unease that the Nipponjika thought it kindly to do as it wished and so leant down and wrapped the coral all up in the velvet seaweed. Within less time than a moment, the little copy had jumped in with a splash and munched up the delicious dande-sealion, head, teeth, and all. The splash sprayed water everywhere, soaking the Nipponjika from its new found top to its bottom, which it had always.

At this moment the Farmer, the Elephant, the Crocodile, and the Hungry Tiger came running over.

'Good evening, pardon me,' panted the Farmer, leaning on the Hungry Tiger for a moment. 'Pardon me, have you seen the mischievous Mouse-deer? We have pursued the trickster here from our homes, where it stole and ate all of my price-winning cucumbers that now won't fetch any price, kicked through my scarecrow, and led my dog to believe it could marry my daughter, which I don't even have, and become a prince, which has made it an incredible nuisance to live with. The dog now refuses to do any of its share around the farm until we discuss a dowry. I've offered it a guest seat at my table to thank it for all the loyal work thus far, but it's no use; it's gotten ahead of itself and can't catch up. What trouble I'm in because of that dastardly Mouse-deer. I must capture it and take it back to explain everything to my dog.' 'Well, that is terrible,' replied the Nipponjika, feeling quite honestly so.

'That is not all,' interposed the Elephant now. 'Do tell us if you know where that little pest of a Mouse-deer is. We have chased it from our woods, where having clumsily fallen into a rather obvious hunters trap hole, it called for my help. Not seeing any other choice, I climbed in thinking that it would be easy enough for me to climb out again, and doing so, that pest of a Mouse-deer jumped up on my back and ran away without further thought. However, having at first jumped about so furiously calling for help, it had loosened the ground making it too soft and crumbly for me to climb out again. I would surely have been shot by the hunters for my ivory had the Crocodile not come my way. The Crocodile and I have made up, you see, for having given me this long trunk. I, in fact, find it useful reaching for juicy fruit, and the Crocodile helped me out before the hunters could come. I must constrain the Mouse-deer and take it back to help harden the ground for any poor animals caught in it in the future.'

Why the nipponjika wears velvet coral on its crown   **95**

'That is an awful story,' commented the Nipponjika, feeling more and more bereaved.

'That is not the end of it,' entered the Crocodile to the discussion. 'Please, won't you point us in the direction of that pranking Mouse-deer? We have been following it from our rivers, where it on one day fed me a stick giving me nasty splinters in my teeth, on the next day taunted me without reason for looking in the water much like a log, and on the third day, embarrassed my whole family and me. That pranking Mouse-deer told me to gather my family in a line so that it could count us for the King. Now, knowing the Mouse-deer's habits, I was sceptical but what if it were true? I couldn't disrespect the King. So we all lined up, when the prankster leapt on our backs and, using us as stepping stones, ran to the opposite side of the river bank. Now, sister Crocodile, who I am ever so close with, won't talk to me from embarrassment, that being the first time she had been mounted. I must seize it and take it home to apologise to my sister and tell her it was not my fault.'

'What an upsetting set of events,' noted the now distressed Nippon-jika.

'But it is far from over,' bemoaned the Hungry Tiger. 'Give us at very least the shifty Mouse-deer's scent track. I beg you. We have been tracking it from our forest, where it gave me permission to try the King's pudding, and so I did and took a big mouthful, but it turned out to be mud. Then having caught it to scold it justly, the shifty Mouse-deer gave me, in form of an apology, permission to hit the King's drum, of which I was suspicious like the Crocodile here, but if it were true I would be losing such an opportunity, and so I did, but it turned out to be a wasp's nest full of wasps that wished to sting me all the way to the river. Catching that shifty Mouse-deer once more to scold it properly, it gave me permission to wear the King's

belt, which truly would have been an honour. But I knew better, and before I could say what I knew, the belt had wrapped itself around me, mostly because it turned out to be the Cobra and bit me squeezing, or at least that is what the Shepherd told me had happened, for I had passed out by then. I must apprehend it and return with it to the King so that it can be suitably scolded once and for all.'

'All of these accounts concern me greatly,' said the Nipponjika, being now in a fix. It believed each story and thought the Mouse-deer should return to their home but, having given its word and being a deer of its word, was bound. 'But can you not see that I am the Mouse-deer grown? I am truly sorry for all the harm I may have caused,' said the Nipponjika, bending its forelegs and tipping its head in supplication.

'Ha,' the four laughed. 'You are no more the Mouse-deer than the Hungry Tiger is the King himself,' said the four assuredly, other than the Hungry Tiger, who was thinking something similar though not the same and had stopped its sentence at 'than'. 'For one thing, the Mouse-deer would not let itself grow to such mighty stature, for it would inconvenience its mischief,' pointed out the Farmer. 'Yes, and neither would the Mouse-deer have a dripping back of soft speckled creamy-white spots, you have clearly been recently splashed, but those beautiful markings are clear enough to see now,' indicated the Elephant. 'Yes, and most importantly, the Mouse-deer does not have anything like such a magnificent velvet coral crown as you do,' continued the Crocodile. 'It is quite clear to us that you are, in all ways that we can see, the Khan of these eastern plains,' finished the Hungry Tiger with a nod.

Not having really paid any attention to all or any of this or possibly having paid it but gotten bored and fidgety again, the Mouse-deer, up to a moment ago still hidden in the marshy water, could not stand sitting or floating still any longer and jumped out with another big splash. 'It is I, the Mouse-deer, you stupids. I can't believe you were fooled for even a second by this larger and stupider version of me,' it said, running off singing its song. And being pursued, chased, followed, and tracked by the four bereft animals behind it, the Nipponjika was left standing there alone once more. It looked down into the waters as the ripples settled and decided that it rather liked the velvety coral on its crown and might well keep it and continued to think over the Meerkats' puzzle.

WHY THE LION GLUED ITS TAIL TO ITS NECK

If by some chance you find yourself somewhere between a curiosity and a wondering on why the Lion has its mane, you may fairly consider asking your elders. Grandparents talk little sense but know more than they let on, so they are often a good place to start. However, it is all too possible if not most likely they will instead not explain why the Lion has anything, but tell you a story of when they once saw a lion, along with a long and rather irrelevant anecdote of what happened after the encounter. So when or if the story ends, you may have forgotten the original question. Do not be fooled. These crafty grandparents are wise to you and have their ways. You could leave breadcrumbs to your original question or tie a string around your finger; either way, perseverance is key. However, for all the questions you have to ask, this is one that can be answered here, without your grandparents, with me. So if you are not yet wily enough to get any real information from the old shrewds, roll over, say uncle, and I will tell you the story of why the Lion has its mane, just so, in truth.

In the Forest, where Wild Beasts live and sturdy trees stump so that even the smallest, most saddest-looking weeping willow should be feared, was the Lion who had found its courage. It didn't know it had found its courage, and in truth, it had had it all along, if you look back, but now it was undoubtedly aware that it had something. However, accounts of the Lion to this point had focussed more on its search for courage than it itself, and so either neglected a thorough description or gave an inthorough one. At this time, when Giant Spiders ate the Wild Beasts of the Forest, however big or small, as they entangled stuck to webs that crisscrossed, hatched over the canopy refracting light so that thousands of small rainbows bathed the forest floor in colour, the Lion's appearance had yet to be altered. At this time, the Lion had no distinctive mane other than the hair that naturally grows around any Wild Beast's neck and had a slender yet powerful body ending with a generous bushy tail. This all was not inexplicable. The Lion would use its tail to brush away the giant spider webs hanging from above. Were it to have a mane instead, then its head would get entangled, and it might well become the spiders' entrée. However, what this meant was that the Lion, already the biggest of its kind, looked much like a colossal squirrel, which didn't help the courage issue and meant that no other Wild Beast of the Forest, however big or small, feared it.

The Lion went on many adventures yet still felt something unsatisfied. So one day, the Lion decided it needed more than just courage, it needed to be loved, respected, and just a little bit feared. It needed to become King of the Forest. The title had in fact been offered to the Lion on one previous adventure, when it unnoticingly, courageously slew a Giant Spider in its sleep, but time had moved on, and offers do not last forever. There were currently two Wild Beasts vying for the position – the biggest and most tailless of the Bandar-log Monkeys, who wished to be a man and a French one, no less, and the Hungry Tiger, who by now had gotten its stripes though that in

truth is another story, and was always hungry, especially desiring a fat baby, but with too grand a conscience would make do with ice-cream, which it felt numbed its teeth and so, in turn, its hunger, for that is where it figured hunger came from.

Already the French Bander-log and Hungry Tiger had begun conversation with the Forest Mouse, as the Hungry Tiger figured, and French Bander-log agreed that if the Wild Beasts of the Forest from the smallest to the biggest thought them fine enough to be King, then it would be so, and they, being the biggest of their kinds, already thought themselves fine enough indeed, which left only the smallest of the Forest Beasts, the Forest Mouse. The Forest Mouse was however very hard to catch, as it was also the fastest mouse in all of the Forest. It wore a red paisley kerchief around its neck and would shout at the top of its voice, 'Go on! Go on! Up! Up!' at the other Beasts climbing the Forest trees as it would run in circles around the sturdy tree stumps, for it was encouraging and cute like that. As no cat, other than perhaps the sleeping Lion, but it was not here yet, could catch the Forest Mouse, it was left to the French Bander-log, who had climbed a tree to get its encouraging attention.

Previous to this, the French Bander-log had lain macaroons and Dijon Mustard all over the floor so as the Forest Mouse, when it got buoyantly excited and started running around cheering the monkey's climb, with its speedy little feet, would get stuck, and the French Bander-log could come back down the tree to retrieve it. All this took a long time, and so by now, the Lion had come to its decision and had gone to find the Hungry Tiger, who was an old and loitering friend.

When the Lion arrived at the Hungry Tiger's cave, it found its friend along with the French Bander-log both raucously pouncing around beating their chests and snarling. 'Go on! Go on!' the Forest Mouse was calling, jumping up and down, clapping, and running in incredibly fast circles inside an overturned empty Dijon Mustard jar. The Lion, thinking the two Wild Beasts were in an incredibly disoriented bout, sunk its chest, then thrust it out along with a cave trembling roar, which caused both large Beasts to stop and look directly at the Lion, who then quite shy of the attention backed off a little and wrapped its face in its bushy tail.

'Ha, Lion of old! Don't fool me with your roar. I thought at first you were a fierce Beast. Now, who of us do you think is fiercest and should be King?'

'Oui, Lion, 'oo?' snarled the French Bander-log, trying to speak through its snarling mouth and scrunched nose to show as many teeth as possible but making it, in fact, difficult to speak at all. Before the Lion could answer, the Forest Mouse was making another speedy racket.

'Yah! Lion!' it called while running still in circles so that in fact it seemed unlikely that it could see the Lion as anything but an orange-golden blur, if at all. 'Up! Up!' the Lion tipped the Dijon Mustard jar the right way, and the Forest Mouse shot up into the Lion's bushy tail.

The two had in actuality met before. Once, when the Lion was out on an adventure, the Forest Mouse had taken camp in its den. So upon the Lion's return, it pulled the boulder door across and fell asleep only to wake up to the excited little Mouse running all over its body and through its tail. With one sleepy swoop, the Lion caught the Mouse in its paw and considered eating it before the Mouse called out, 'Go on! Go on!' This had disturbed the Lion to no end, as no Mouse should want to be eaten, so the Lion had kept the Mouse in its tail safely for a while before its next adventure came about, and while the Forest Mouse had resided there the Lion always gave it some of its share of food and milk, which wasn't too much to begin with anyway.

'Oobee doo,' the French Bander-log continued. 'I am ze most feared, as I can walk like An'omme,' and rose on its hind legs to start wad-dling around with its much larger forearms swinging back and forth. Now none of them had actually seen An'omme walk, though they could imagine such a grounded thing possibly shaking and swaying in such a way, so gasped with impressed fear. 'It is I 'oo can also talk like An'omme,' claimed the French Bander-log. Now again none of them had heard An'omme talk, and in truth, they didn't know what

An'omme was, though this seemed less plausible. Surely, the Hungry Tiger thought, An'omme would talk with a thicker smokier voice. Or surely, thought the Lion, An'omme would talk with a more hurried gratier voice, for that's the imagery the name inspired.

'That was horrendous,' commented the Hungry Tiger, though at that time 'horrend' was probably a milder more casual word, indeed it had no 'p's or 'q's so could not have been too formal, and so none took offence to this. 'No, no. I am the most feared, for, I am symmetrical. Look!' it said lining up face to face with the Lion, so it could see the Hungry Tiger in two halves as if framed in a dull-composed portrait. 'Two thin fiery eyes, two creepy shoulders, two dreadful front paws, and two dreadful back. Admit it, old friend, my symmetry is fearful.' The Lion looked upon the Hungry Tiger carefully. It was true it had two eyes, it had two shoulders, there were indeed two front paws, and yes, if you looked behind them closely enough, there sat two back paws also. Having never noticed this symmetry before, the Lion began to quiver with fear until it spotted a patch of the Hungry Tiger's coat stained with ice-cream. It checked the other side, noted it was not stained so, and therefore being not symmetrical at all, was no more fearful than any other animal.

The whole time the great Beasts had been deliberating, whiskers and glimpses of red paisley kerchiefs were darting out from the corners of the Lion's tail and dashing back in again accompanied by snickers, sniggles, and faint calls to go on and up, muffled in the dense fur. And so the Lion stepped forward.

'Ha, you sink it iz you 'oo iz ze most feared? Wiz your bushy tail. Ha,' laughed the Bander-log, now especially getting into its French. 'Look, old friend, I do believe the ape has a point. With that tail, it is hard to take you all too seriously,' the Tiger added.

With this the Forest Mouse, possibly because it recalled the Lion's kindness when it gave it some food and milk instead of eating it as Lions do, or perhaps because it had gotten dizzy from running in circles and simply stumbled off, fell from the Lion's tail, grabbed a pair of nail clippers on the Hungry Tiger's side table and dove back into the Lion's bushy tail. The three great Wild Beasts could hear clips and claps and that things, according to the Forest Mouse, were going up, until finally, all the bushy tail fur fell down onto the floor. The Forest Mouse had sheared it all off, leaving a handsome slick tail with a small tuft at the end big enough for the Forest Mouse to fit in and run around in now very little circles, but this was no time for that yet. The Forest Mouse then, and this time quite clearly intentionally, jumped down and grabbed some macaroons and Dijon Mustard from the French Bander-log's bag and, mulching them into a paste by pattering its feet and tail all over them with fantastic speed, found itself left with a mulched paste but not despairing, it slathered it all over the Lion's neck. The Dijon Mustard, having such a yellow-brown spicy smell, made the Lion's whiskers twitch and tremble until it sneezed almightily, with which all the hair puffed up, covering the Lion's neck and held glued on by the paste.

As the French Bander-log and Hungry Tiger looked through the cloud of falling hair, they saw before them not the same Lion as before, but a Lion to be feared, the biggest of its kind, with now, around its neck, a distinguishing mane feature, as worthy of the King of the Forest. So the Lion was ceremoniously given the title and its share, befitting that of a King, became a little larger, though some of it will always go on and up to the little Forest Mouse in the tuft at the end of its tail.

WHY THE ANGLERFISH
CARRIES A LANTERN

If, as many people do, you find yourself wondering how the Anglerfish glows in the dark, you may decide to conduct an extensive
search into the matter. Such a search would assuredly reveal many an
explanation, such like the glowing light attracts the Anglerfish's food
to it, making food preparation a thing of the past. Clearly, this would
be desirable for all of us, especially those hard-working parents with
hungry mouths, attached to hungry bodies, to feed. However, how
does the glowing light get its power? We all know that there are no
electric sockets under the water because water is a conductor, possibly the greatest of all conductors as bus conductors only go along
one route, but water goes in all directions. Well, the lack of a real
explanation is not surprising, so don't feel duped by your search. The
fact is all this came about so far away that not even the greatest tel-
escope could have seen it. So permit me to recount the explanation
as it occurred, just so, in truth.

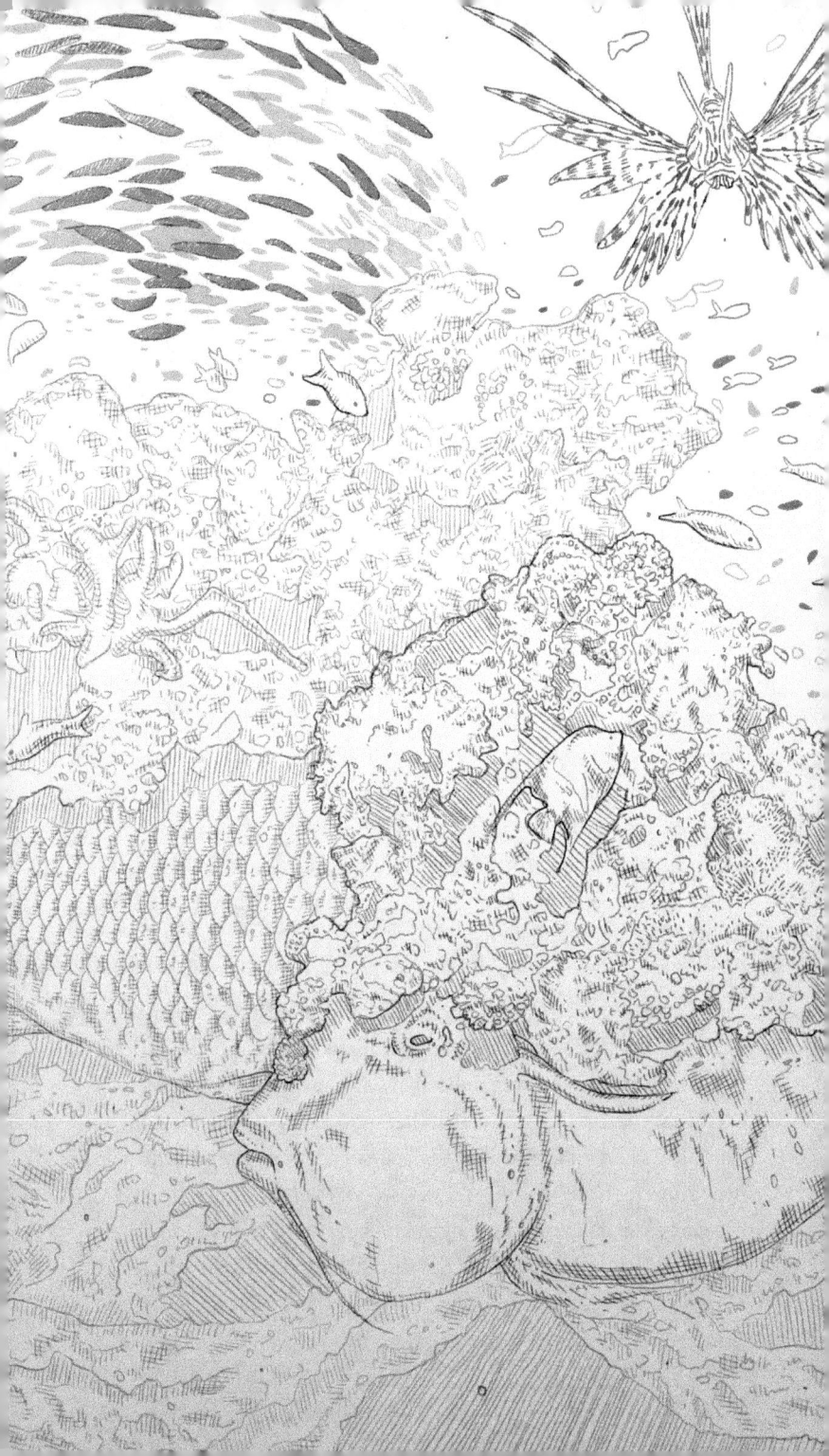

Deep deep beneath the Myradean Sea, below where the old Limpets break the waves, below where the Crab collects pebbles and seaweed to make its nest, below the coral forests where dwarf Goby Fish and their pygmy cousins sway with the deep water tide, below where no tide sways, far below the shade of the Octopus' garden, where there is no shade at all because there is no light, and without one you cannot have the other, below here, where time lies dormant, and great goliath sea-monsters only wake for when the earth itself shudders and below this, deeper than any sunken valley goes, there is a city, lost to all of those that never knew it was.

In this city of carefully cobbled mosaic streets with images that tell stories so old only these ancient stones can tell them, of high sturdy walls of stone each intricately engraved with patterns that once carried meaning when time was perhaps measurable, live creatures so baffling in design and nature that the minds of those up on land would not conceive them and so eyes could not see them, though it would not matter anyhow, as it is so dark that even the Cat, with its disappearing eyes that absorb and reflect light, would step back thinking it were moving forward. Here where the right way is up, and the up side is down sleeps the Anglerfish. The spiny Anglerfish, with its large downturned mouth, bulbous head so that it appears to have in fact no body and spiny spines that shoot from its sides and end where fins ought to be.

Here also sleeps the Viperfish and its comb-needle teeth that scarcely eats but lives on tiny disappointed feelings that slump to the deep. And here slowly and methodically wash the bioluminescent Lanternfish, the Fireflies of the sea, that sparkle like distant stars for a moment then disappear into the blackness once more. And here lies the Sabertooth fish, which cannot see forward but only up to spot its prey, as it floats unknowingly, breaking any streams of bioluminescence that rain down like the sun through a thick forest canopy.

Here, in the all-but-dead city rests the Ladyfish. Here she rests for one aeon and half an epoch. Here she rests quietly and still but not inert, for it is said that at the Oceanic equinox, when the moon has reached its zenith over the equator, and its push and pull of the waves are equal, forcing a nostalgic stillness over the ocean, she wakes.

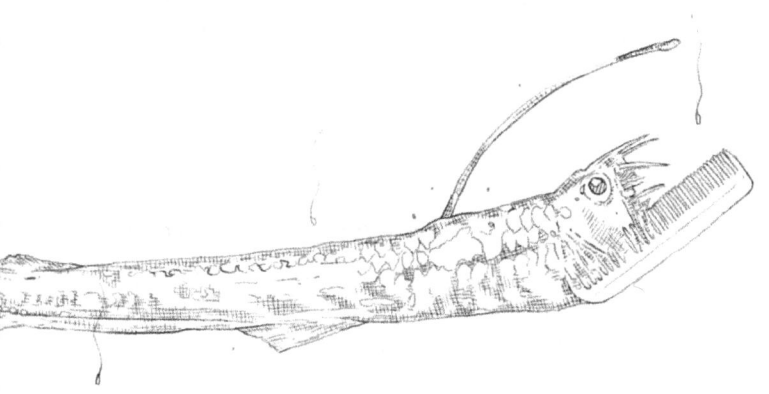

The story goes, as it is said, that the young Weaving Lady Fish wove beautifully through the florescent coloured coral, fins soft and thin as silk gliding around her speckled golden figure. That the Weaving Lady had a father, who lived to watch this embroidered dance. However, the young Weaving Lady was torn, as it was easy to tear such delicate thread, for to dance and please her father meant to forfeit finding love and to seek love meant to abandon her father.

Her father could sense her little heart tearing, and concerned, he arranged a meeting with the sageful Cow-heard, a perennial Lord, who having heard anyone's disheartenings could inspirit one through essential medical herbs. But when the Weaving Lady and Cow-heard Lord met, they fell deeply in love in an instant and soon promised that love eternally. However, from putting their feelings to words, it became all the Weaving Lady could weave so that only words and no dance would occupy her mind, and it became all the Cow-heard could hear so that its ears closed to the cows and pleas of others.

The father was upset by this and forbade them to meet again and separated them by the great Ocean currents. The Weaving Lady became dispirited so that only the Cowherd Lord could cure. The father, who cared for his daughter dearly, was moved by such love and allowed the two to meet every aeon and half an epoch when the Oceanic equinox calms the Ocean currents to a still whisper. At least this is all as it is said to have happened.

This is where our story begins, in an instant. In an instant unknown to time, the water began to calm and settle, and the great Ocean currents unruffled their feathers until all stopped breathless. The Anglerfish was the first to open its eyes. The Anglerfish had, since it could remember, been charged with the most important job of plotting the path of the procession taking the Weaving Lady across the Ocean currents to meet her love would go, a job that suited it perfectly as the city had so many great walls with great corners of great angles. The Anglerfish took pride in being the only Angler, and in its duty, but having planned the path, would follow the procession from behind and never ever see the young Weaving Lady, despite wanting to so dearly.

So the Anglerfish planned a quite spectacular path, which twisted and bent down streets of overhanging Salmonberries with their salmon-orange fruit and tart red Cowberries, for they reminded the Weaving Lady of her love eternally. A path that passed the ornate shrines which would be lifted on palanquins to join the procession. A path that turned corners at angles, some sharp, some soft, some steep, some shallow, and all well-formed.

Then woke the Viperfish, with its long body that would slide through the hooks in the shrines to lift the palanquins upon its back as a true pole bearer. Dressing in an imprinted festival coat tied by a soft obi sash and with a colourful hachimaki headband stopping its sweat drip down as a symbol of perseverance, for the shrines in the dark were not light at all.

And woke the Sabertooth fish, which swimming flat, would carry huge drums that then looked as if they were floating independently. Fastening the cork tops of rice wine jugs to its teeth, with which it would beat against the drums, making the musical rhythm to which all in the procession would swim.

However, as the Sabertooth tried to fasten the cork tops of rice wine, a pleasure it had looked forward to for an aeon and half an epoch as the cork had soaked up a lot of wine into its juicy bark, it could not find the corks or its teeth, for it realised all was entirely dark. Usually, before the Sabertooth fish woke, the bioluminescent Lantern Fish would be streaming around, flickering light that bathed and reflected across the mosaic street floors so that all sparkled. However, no Lantern Fish was to be found. Perhaps, it is said by some, they woke too early and led a radiant soundless procession through the city before going back to sleep. Or perhaps, it is said by others, they left the city as beacons to bear the torch of the old Limpet's games but found themselves lost as they neared the surface, for with the sun beating down the deep-sea fireflies disappeared into the light. Either way, if the young Weaving Lady woke with the Cowherd Lord on her mind and could see no lights and hear no drums, she would be ill to the heart, and this had to be avoided as all the creatures in the city liked the young Weaving Lady and her beautiful embroidered dance.

One Lantern Fish had though luckily left one lantern behind, but when lit, it would only shine a dim light that could not illuminate the whole procession. Were the Viperfish or Sabertooth Fish to carry the lantern, they would still not be able to see clearly enough to follow the correct path; besides, they had to carry shrines and drums. In fact, no creature in the procession could carry the lantern. The whole city was in a dark hysteria as though black death had fallen upon them, for if the young Weaving Lady could not see her love, she would surely die as young lovers inevitably do, with a sip of poisonous heartache in the night.

Amidst this panic, the Anglerfish approached the council which had formed to discuss the matter. The Anglerfish swam slowly to the front stage that had been erected from crustacean shells sunken and hardened with pressure to the deep deep. The Anglerfish stood, and all eyes were on it, for which the Sabertooth had to move to below the stage. As the route planner, it acutely knew all the angles it beseeched, even the most obtuse ones, and whether in the dimmest light or not, it would always take the right angle.

The council and indeed the whole city agreed that the Anglerfish should lead the way, so they tied the floats and drums and palanquins bound with long strands of kelp, and they placed the lantern on the top of the longest spine on the Anglerfish, right over its head.

As the young Weaving Lady woke, she did not feel uneasy in the dusky light. The procession led through the streets, the head shimmered with shrines and beating drums and the veiled young Weaving Lady dancing embroidered behind. The whole city, singing their folk chants together, took the young Weaving Lady across the still ocean currents.

Now it is clear why the Anglerfish carried a lantern, so you may stop reading here if you wish, but it leaves the problem of tense in our question, and very few like being left tense. The Anglerfish went back to sleep with the rest of the city only found by those who never knew what they were looking for, for how could you know before you found it? And it is difficult to know why the Anglerfish kept the lantern and carries it to this day. But I suppose, as I'm occasionally inclined to do, that the Anglerfish with such reflexes found itself constantly turning. As we are all aware, the angle is only the amount of turn between two arms, and having no arms, the Anglerfish could never end its turn and was forced to carry the lantern all the way until the present tense and inevitably onwards. Or at least that is what I suppose.

The Ladybird and
The Hummingbird

A lovely little Ladybird,
leaping leaf to leaf,
fetched a hum that could be heard,
but ushered off too brief,
approached a petalled poplar plant
soft melody in sway,
and tunefully abjured a grant
of sugared milky way.
Bestowed, so with a silken pat
the Ladybird tipped feathered hat,
turned to pursue its former course,
stopped startled by a flitting source.

'Oh Hummingbird,' the insect hummed,
'How do you do old chum?'
And danced and hummed and, with wings, strummed
on a dendritic drum.
Their carnal dance brought eventide
so weary, they retired
to set a stove and sit astride,
and eat what e'er desired.
They reasoned on the Summer's gloam
and why the grudging Sun won't roam
with the Moon, but scrambles down,
leaves in the lurch Night's dressing gown.

The Ladybird soft turned a query
and threw a ginger look,
'Dear Hummingbird are you but bleary
from the Day's strain shook?
Our coterie of course is charming,
witty, downright neighbourly,
I've no intent to be alarming,
but can't you hum quite ably?
In ebbing glow, we sang "Brows-blow"
and many woodland tunes we know.
Though you danced and strummed the drum,
I don't believe you did once hum.'

'Oh Ladybird, I burn forlorn,
dipped in the Styx by throat.
To harmonise with zephyrs bourn,
but cannot hum a note.
I umm 'n' err 'n' pipe 'n' purr,
I caw 'n' crow 'n' croak,
with Mephistopheles confer
on this Faustian joke.
A perfumed rose with laud replete
by any name may smell as sweet,
but name a scentless poppy: 'rose',
just dress it ready to repose.'

'The Mockingbird first harks the ditty
of a feathered-fowl,
and mimics meter well and witty,
from his name, won't cowl.
Fly fast! The Dragonfly sprys by,
though trials a tread quite lame,
and with his dragon eyes does spy,
how fitting is his name.
The fates that stitched my tapestry
with heedfulness gone absentee
named me thus: The Hummingbird,
but with no hum, named absurd.'

'That lucky Meadowlark stands stark
atop its meadow mound,
and 'round its mouth a chatter-mark
from all its larking 'round.
With chiselled bill kept tapered sharp,
The Woodpecker quick could
peck a hole in cliff face scarp,
were it made up of wood.
And on the tree, it drills and drums,
but never utters breath of hum,
for Hummingbird is not its name
and not to hum is not its shame.'

The Ladybird then sighed a sigh
that flit the soft stove flame,
'Your discontent is proper, aye,
a valid troubled claim.
It's cruel your title doesn't suit,
if we could but reword,
till all the benign beasts salute
The Dancing-Strummingbird.
But there are worse names, you'll agree,
let's momentarily take me:
I'm not from bird, but insect clan,
and what is more, I am a man.'

WHY THE LADYBIRD BURNT
ITS BACK SEVEN TIMES

If you look closely at many an animal, you will find it has a pattern on its coat. That pattern might be a stripe or two, though one lone stripe is rather less common, a few daubs or a whole spangle. The Ladybird, an animal that wears its famous patterned coat very well indeed, has spots. The Ladybird doesn't have too many spots nor too few, but quite the right number of spots, about seven, which might lead you to believe it were all intentional. Indeed if you were to ask any well-thunk adult, they would surely agree, and even the Ladybird, if you could talk to it anymore, might politely confirm your conclusion. However, the Ladybird, being polite no doubt, would also be being avoiding a rather embarrassing story on its behalf. So if you asked the Ladybird to explain why it has those spots, it might well try to avoid the discussion, and if you asked the same well-thunk adult, they may well too, for it is not an easy question to answer, unless your answer is that you don't know, which is easy enough to say yet sometimes feels so difficult to say in fact. It is not an easy question to answer, unless you know the answer, which, as it has come about, I do. So with your leave, though please don't go anywhere, I will recount to you the experiences of the Ladybird as they took place, just so, in truth.

The sun was quite used to shining, that being its only recourse, on the same dewy blades of grass that had been hardened by the morning frost. The frost rose, as it tended to on Winter mornings, across the hilltops, their stacks of hay with the unaccompanied hoe or pitchfork projecting out and up to the tips of each grass bristle and off, climbing up the occasional tree foot before the sun warmed it back to sleep. Here, where patchwork fields lay unsmoothed across the horizon to make a quilt of lush greens sombering into burnt golds, here, without the cover of the forest trees or water deep, the smaller animals reigned. The birds hopped through the grasses, chirped, and flittered off as though playing a coy game of cat-and-mouse, of which the rules were only truly known to them, though it certainly didn't involve a true cat or true mouse. The fields did, however, reveal here the paths of field mice that scuttled about making small alluring tunnels through the overhanging golden stalks. Here, the insects crawled and fluttered and buzzed alone or in groups with direction or none, but so much so that any larger animal that found itself here would also find itself soon lying on its back with heavy eyes folding down to the gentle hum of the hillside. Here was a place that simultaneously made apparent how time moved everything, while also slowing time to no more than picture frames, making it very hard to tell when here really was.

Here lived the Ladybird, inside a hollowed-out acorn dropped by a passing bird or mouse long ago, and it thought itself very normal. The Ladybird had a queer name, that it would admit, and in fact what to call it at all was quite difficult to say. It was clearly not a bird, it was in fact also not a true bug, but at best a tiny beetle, and not a very interesting one at that. With its small rounded body covered with a blackish-green shell, it was often hard to see in the newer grasses. However, the Ladybird was to have quite an unnormal experience that would change its tone distemporarily and unconditionally.

One day, when the sun was still chasing the frost across the field, wafting up a cool breeze, there was a knocking on the Ladybird's acorn. Wiping the sleep from its eyes and going to the door, the Ladybird was soon looking down at a four-winged Zoraptera. It would not be a huge surprise to me were you to say you were unfamiliar with the Zoraptera, for you hardly look similar, so it is clear that you could not be of the same family, and for its order was in fact to contain only one family, and as a result of following its order, it kept much to itself. It may have also been a recluse, as with the Ladybird, as it was a little abashed by its name, which meant literally 'purely wingless' yet it had at occasions, including this one, two pairs of spanned wings. If this second perhaps happens to be more frequently true than once per hap, it may also explain why the Zoraptera went casually by the name of the 'Angel insect'.

The Angel insect was munching on a fungal spore when it looked up at the Ladybird and spoke.

'Nom, and behold, you will con-nom-nom bear a son,' was the distinguishable heart of the Angel insect's message.

'Please enunciate,' asked the Ladybird, 'I can't understand a word you say.' The Angel insect swallowed the large spore, coughed a bit, and started again.

'Hand me, hold your wool, hic,' it hiccupped, 'a cover or something, I can't bear the sun.' The Ladybird, having nothing but the shell on its back, said as much. Now there being some confusion and miscommunication, the Angel insect accepted the shell, though at least apparently appreciating the generosity, and offered a switch. In exchange, the Angel insect gave the Ladybird a red coat and flew away. 'Why wouldn't the lad have just worn this nice coat?' thought the Ladybird and, being chilled, pulled it over its head. Looking at the distorted reflection on the acorn wall, the Ladybird saw why – there was a big black stain or burn mark. It had been duped by its possibly intoxicated morning visitor, but ho-hum, the Ladybird continued with its day.

The Ladybird in truth had a breakfast picnic planned with a few other beetles and true bugs, all of whom were required to bring something to eat. So the Ladybird began going about its preparations. The Ladybird was a proud locavore, only cooking with local, native ingredients – native grasses, native corn, native hop, to make a native brew. While the Ladybird was preparing, however, one hop bound right out of the bubbling pot and onto the Ladybird's coat, burning a second delicious black mark onto it. 'Oh, this nativity really does try my patience, but ho-hum,' cussed the Ladybird, and it left its house with the picnic dish in hand.

At the picnic, all food was laid out on a big picnic mat made of a dock leaf, for all insects knew then and indeed probably are still aware now that the dock leaf was the finest of doctors around and could surely help with any sting, with which many insects were inflicted, or burn, which the Ladybird quite literally sorely needed. But word in these humming fields soon spread, and before long, three Magpies arrived at the picnic.

'We hear that the Ladybird has made a delicious broth. Let us join you. We have brought picnic gifts,' so naturally, the insects asked what gifts were brought.

'I', spoke the first Magpie, 'have brought a golden kiwi I stole from the farmer's wife's pantry.' The insects admired the Magpie's honesty, despite everything being rather golden in the fields already.

'I', spoke the second Magpie, 'have brought an aromatic raisin.' What made the raisin aromatic was unclear so easily visible but unfortunately not explained here, though to be frank, the scent was the best they had ever smelt. To be as honest as the Magpies thus far, the insects had never even imagined they'd smelt a raisin of such incense and were delighted by it.

'…meh,' shrugged the third Magpie, who hadn't thought to bring a gift, and it swooped down to grab some of the Ladybird's broth.

Now in the fields, once all lush green but presently burnt gold, a big black Magpie was rather easy to see coming but was also rather intimidating. In a panic, very close to what the insects had originally come for in fact, though only being a few letters short of a picnic, letters which quite possibly had been 'miss-placed' by the local postage system, the insects desperately struggled to hide the delicious broth. 'Mag-eye!' shouted one insect either because its mouth was as full as the Angel insect's had been earlier that morning or because it could only see one of the Magpie's big eyes. Whichever the case, the whole kerfuffle ended with the broth being knocked over and spilt. The Ladybird tumbled back and fell down on a burning soufflé, scorching its new red coat a third time. But 'ho-hum,' said the Ladybird.

Dejected by the loss of the earthy blend, the insects cleared the dock leaf, which held its liquids well, and poured what was remaining into a tiny chalice made from a small mushroom cap. Their spirits all lifted again as they passed the chalice around, each taking a small sip. They danced, especially the Jitterbug, who became particularly twitchy after a little drink, and sang around a campfire so that the breakfast picnic went on all day and into the evening.

They danced around the fire, sparks flying this way and that, late into the night even, until the Flea had the genius idea of making the last drops of broth into jellied marsh-mellow pieces. The Flea, having come directly from the market, was dressed in a buttoned waistcoat ever so smartly, so all insects thought it must have good ideas and did just as it said. They then held the jellied marsh-mellows over the fire, but the Ladybird, who was trying it first, held it slightly too long, and the drop burst right onto its new coat making yet a fourth black spot. 'Darn,' swore the Ladybird, 'this is getting ridiculous. But ho-hum.' With which the Ladybird and all the other insects fell asleep around the fire.

The following morning, the sun, doing as it was inclined to once again, woke the drowsy insects with groggy heads and heavy though entirely satisfied bodies. This, unfortunately, was a pain they knew well, as insects and animals over many hilltops had experienced it before, about which the dock leaf could do little. This pain was what the animals in these humming fields referred to as a 'hangover', mostly because the only remedy they'd heard of was to hang one's head over a glass of water and drink it backwards or something, though that may have been the remedy for hiccups. Anyway, the best way to name a problem is by the solution so as to never forget, hence the word 'hiccup' or 'high-cup'. But instead of hanging their heads over water, it was decided that a nice fragrance would calm their heads and lighten their bodies. The insects took the aromatic raisin and last drop of marsh-mellow broth and burnt them over the still glowing fireplace. The fragrance lifted up and up as though ascending to the sun to help the sun lighten its body and then possibly the day.

'The sun did not dance and sing all night,' complained the insects with reasonable cause.

'It is we who need this aromatic pick-me-up,' the Ladybird said, still lying on its back, addressing the smartly dressed Flea, though now its bow had been loosened and waistcoat unbuttoned, so it wasn't quite as smart.

'Yeah,' supported the Flea, with little other inspirational ingenuity worth mentioning.

'No, no. Pick me up! If you give me a boost, I'll catch the smell as it rises.'

'Ah, climb on.' And the Flea lifted the Ladybird up. However, the sun knowing all too well that it hadn't been dancing and singing but now having been tempted by the fragrance and seeing how much the insects wanted it only exacerbating the matter, shone as hard as it could on the Ladybird, burning a new fifth spot on its now old red coat so that the Ladybird couldn't bear it and had to climb back down again.

'Well, let the sun have it,' muttered the Ladybird, 'and I hope the spice tickles until it sneezes and loses it daily path. And ho-hum!'

All the insects soon spread out a hearty lunch made up of the cold meats and bread from the day before, but before they could start cutting the cheese, the dock leaf began to shake. The insects, sitting cross-legged, began to vibrate backwards until they all rolled over and off the leaf, which was lifted into the air.

'Holy Moley,' exclaimed the Ladybird, as the Mole stuck out its whiskered snout, nipping the air.

'Beg your pardon,' the Mole croaked, fumbling around all clumsily. 'I just came from the Squirrel, who burnt down a whole field,' it said brushing itself off. 'Imagine making a cross bun with hot buttons, entirely impractical!' it continued as scorched buttons popped off it here and there, with insects jumping out of the way to avoid them. The Ladybird, however, could not jump anyway, as it had tumbled onto its back once again and was struggling to turn itself the right way up. 'Can I lend you a hand little, buddy?' asked the Mole, extending a finger to push the Ladybird the right way up. However, nails still scorching from digging through burnt soil, the Mole burnt a sixth black hole right into the Ladybird's red coat, making it tumble over again and inspiriting the Ladybird into a veritable passion.

'Agh, this is not at all ho-hum but in fact, rather frustrating,' exclaimed the Ladybird, though soon calming down, for the Ladybird was generally a calm little beetle. 'But is there no haven where we can eat a meal in peace without burning my coat?' urged the Ladybird. All feeling largely sympathetic, they decided to create a burn-free haven. They collected the most fire-proof sticks, being the dry and bristly sticks that could most easily catch alight, for that certainly would prove fire, and built a little hut. However, half-way through completing the haven, the Ladybird began to smoke. Not being a heavy smoker or even a smoker at that, though certainly being alight, it came as a shock to everyone. The Ladybird had, you see, become hot under the collar from the work and had in all probability sparked by its lapse of frustration. So when finally the water bugs had doused out the flames, the Ladybird looked under its collar to find a seventh burnt black spot on its red coat and with a deep sigh, 'ho-hum,' said the Ladybird.

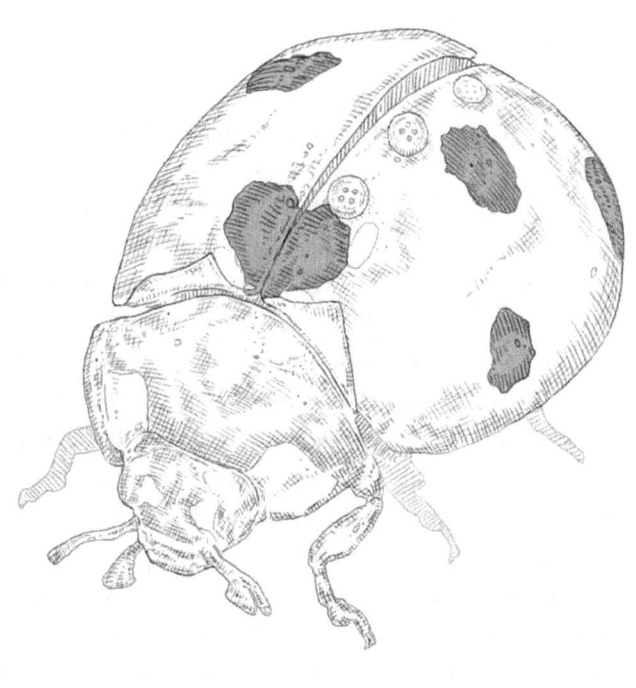

WHY THE PUFFIN BENT THE SWAN'S NECK

There is no question not worth asking. But some questions are worth more than others. In fact, I believe you could make a veritable living from selling some questions. Though, I suppose you would need to prove the value of a question without giving it away for free first, so allow me to try. The Puffin and the Swan are both birds, to which I presume you would agree. And birds have taken wings, which flip and flap, something I imagine you've seen. These wings help the bird jump very far distances, and even over seas, a fact your teacher may have confirmed already. Then that leads us back to the Puffin and Swan, who don't seem to be able to jump very far at all, and leads us directly to my valuable point in question, why does the Swan have a bent neck? If you also appreciate the value in this question, you, I hope, can acknowledge its merit for itself alone. However, it just so seems that this is a question of which I am aware of the answer. So, if you believe that hearing the answer to a question by no means devalues it, then spend a moment to listen to why the Swan, of all birds, got its bent neck, just so, in truth.

Fore atop an age, far far gone, here lodged the Puffin and there the Swan. Nevertheless, this juncture begins an age and a day gone, and the Puffin and Swan are still, as you would say, in the dark, despite it actually being a brisk, bright, and clamorous day. This day was much like any other – the birds were shining, shimmering their gloss feathers in the fountain; the sun was singing, whistling the wind back and forth, for the exercise was good for it, and most, though not all, of the animals were engaged in quite a frolic.

In these times, there were two most popular sports that most of, though not all, the animals loved to play. The first was a local version of tiddlywinks, which they called tweedlywinks, which may be accounted for in other writings but shan't be here, though it was without reservation, full of the joys of Spring, howbeit played in the new Winter. The other was indeed a sport to be played as the trees leaf and flower buds unfold, especially on days such as this when the wind was exceptionally animated, as it too wished to join the hulla-balloo, who was, in turn, putting on its shorts ready to join the game of 'Have only gone where all should head', as it was inexplicably called. Note that to explain the origins of this title there have been a few theories, the best of which is that the literally descriptive title was mistakenly taken from a random sentence in the original rulebook rather than from the title on the title page, but since no one has seen the rule book and even less know what the rules are, we can't be sure of anything.

Have only gone where all should head or otherwise known sociably as 'Hogwash', for sometimes or more often than not, it also involved the Hog being washed, was a non-contact sport by its official nature, yet those hard of sight were permitted to wear them unofficially, and in fact it was a common theme of discussion between players. Each side consisted of any number of players, depending on how many were in appropriate shape to play, which was examined before the game by making a chest in the day's designated shape and seeing which animals could fit snuggly inside. After this, the teams were decided, which was done by lining up atop the Floret Hill, sprayed with Blue-lace flowers and Button Funrays of a distinctive yellow, lying arms stretched, and rolling down. If the player stops at the bottom wrapped more in blue lace, then they join one team and are called a crochet, whereas if the player stops at the bottom more fastened with yellow buttons, then they join another team and are otherwise known as a catch. So, on this frumptuous day, a game of Hogwash was underway, and today it was especially exciting as the teams had an even number of players for the first time since when one unnamed player, the Squirrel, who was planning on making a cross bun laced with brandy, picked a hot button and ended up burning down the whole Floret Hill's side, so that when the animals rolled down to the bottom they were wrapped and fastened more in nothing and neither team had any players.

But now we have come to an age ago, and there was a himmer-hammering on the door of the Puffin's house and a bitter-battering on the door of the Swan's home.

'Come quick you both,' a voice cried.

'What is it you want, you clattery Baboon?' asked the Puffin, having come to its doorstep.

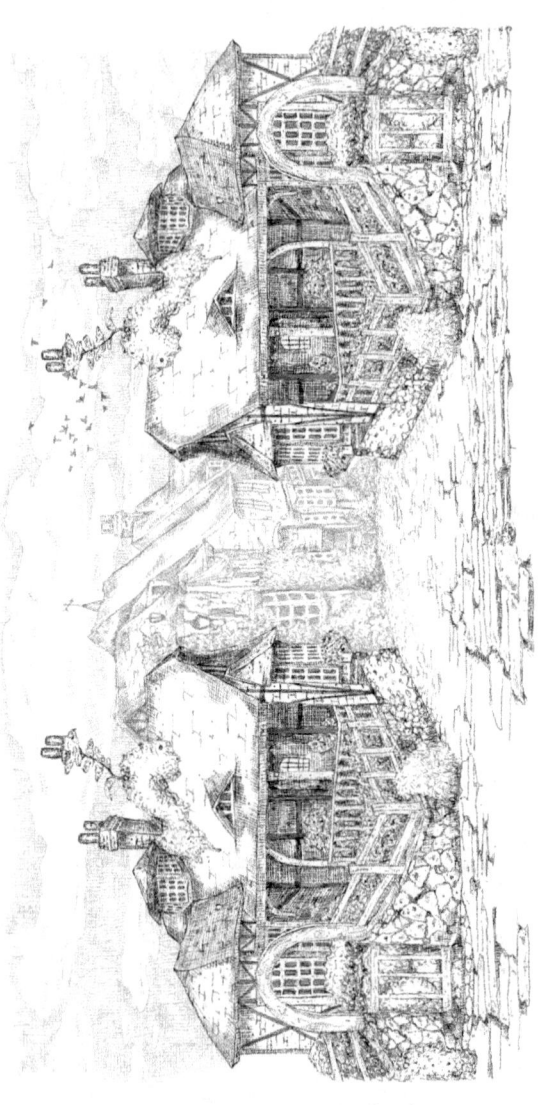

'Yes, though I loath to agree with that pretentious Puffin, why are you hollering so, you lumbering Baboon?' agreed the Swan. This confused the caller to no end, for it was the Alpaca and wasn't and had never been a baboon; however, it soon noticed the two were clearly mid-dining, with mouths stuffed full of grapes and sausages, so probably intended on calling it a buffoon, which it had been once or twice, though not on this occasion.

'I shan't help you,' called the Puffin, before listening to any explanations.

'And I shan't even harder,' called the Swan, the two glaring directly at each other and ignoring the Baboon, who was actually the Alpaca, completely.

'Well, then I shan't hardly help.'

'Then I shall help the appropriate amount.'

'Then I shall help even harder,' and the two continued this while reaching for their bowler hats, canes, and pipes and slamming their doors as hardly as possible behind them. Before the conversation could get back to them deciding not to help, they were at the game, and it was a mess.

<Right, so look left before crossing the street.

The yellow buttoned Gibbon was leading a group of lace crotchets in a catchy dance, a little like the hockey-pockey but involving a lot faster twirling. The Grasshopper, who was clearly a catch, had made a grass slipper and was trying it on every yellow crotchet before it would choose a dance partner for the hoedown, though the Koi, being so abashed by nature, was making it hard for the Grasshopper to put the grass slipper on, as it skittishly wriggled with every touch.

The Goose and its stream of little goslings were, all but one, dressed in blue lace and arching overlooking intently at something. While one gosling, no uglier than the rest, but buttoned up in yellow, was leapfrogging this way and that, trying to see what the others were looking at. This had attracted the attention of the Frog, who also started hopping, which had caught the eye of the Rabbit, who with its stream-lined head unencumbered by lofty ears was positively bounding around, though this was typical of the Rabbit, who always seemed to be rushing, bound somewhere or other.

Animals were all sorts of places doing all sorts of bizarrities.

'Can you see what is going on?' the Baboon, who was forgetting it was originally an Alpaca, asked rhetorically.

'Yes, yes. Though where are the Tattlers?' responded the Puffin. 'Indeed, indeed. Though where are the Tattletailers?' responded the Swan. The two, still looking more at each other than where they were walking, used their canes to find their way, which occasionally hit the Baboon, who had now forgotten how to spit like an Alpaca entirely. Ducking to miss the swing of one cane, it replied, 'at the water's edge.'

At the water's edge were two incredibly excited animals, clambering all over each other.

'You see? In a fit of ingenuity, the crotchets wrapped their Tattler in a napkin and threw it into the water.'

'Yes, yes,' replied the Puffin. 'No doubt because it was drowsy.'

'Right. And the catches buttoned their Tattler in a sweater and hurled it in after.'

'Indeed, indeed,' responded the Swan, 'no doubt because it was nervous.'

'And now the game cannot end until both or one of either are retrieved for the Tattletailers to tag.'

Now it was immediately apparent to both the Puffin and the Swan what needed to be done, so they both planted their canes in the sand to lean against and started filling their respective pipes.

'What are you doing?' asked the Baboon, who had by now resolved to being the Baboon.

'You need someone to go into the water to fetch the Tattlers, yes,' said the Puffin while puffing on its pipe.

'You need someone to go into the water, yet you ask two birds, indeed,' said the Swan, swabbing the soot from its pipe.

'But you are the only two animals here that aren't involved in some way or other in the game. How can one be expected to twirl and swim at the same time?'

'I shan't do anything,' wheezed the Puffin, now in a cloud of smoke. 'I cannot swim.'

'And I shan't even harder,' gasped the Swan, now daubing its pipe in the water to get the dregs. 'I, likewise, cannot swim.'

'Well, then I shan't hardly do anything.'

'Then I shall do anything the appropriate amount.'

'Then I shall do anything even harder.'

Both were fervently shouting and waving their pipes and canes while removing their bowler hats, stretching, and edging towards the water.

The Swan jumpflapped into the water, which was so cold that its, up to now regularly lengthed, neck shot up and stayed that way as though the head being farther from the water made it less cold, and goosebumps, very inappropriately, ran all over its now stiff neck. The Puffin, however, dipping one foot into the water and shivering back, ran from the water and out of sight.

The Swan paddled around for a moment and seeing the Tattlers at the bottom of the water, one in a napkin and the other in a sweater, thrust its goosebumps, followed directly by its head, into the water, and stretched to reach them. But at this inopportune moment, a strong gust of wind rolled past, for it was still exceptionally animated, and lifted the Swan from behind so much so that it toppled forward into a showery roly-poly. Soaked and now freezing, its neck was stiffer and longer than ever. But the Swan, being of the character of someone that would stick their neck out to help someone, or at least, to help someone harder than the Puffin, once again stuck its neck straight out into the water. It stretched and stretched and was able to slowly start nudging the Tattlers with its bill-tip towards the shallower water. At this point, the Puffin reappeared at the water's edge with the rather contentious Crab under its wing.

'Unwing me, you imbecile,' yawped the Crab. 'I must get back to my miming before these ridiculous Lemmings lose interest.' And sure enough a line of Lemmings, all tied together by threads of blue lace, were following in their steps, chitter-chattering with their eyes all big and hopeful. The Puffin released the Crab by the water and turning from it, said in the loudest and most pompous voice it could muster,

'This makes me call to mind the Squirrel, who quite rightly once thought the pine forests on the land far superior to those coral forests of the ocean. But now that I have seen you, I realise I was mistaken to bring you, and you are clearly no Crab but in fact the fat Lobster.' Hearing this, the Crab, not being able to reach the Puffin's ears from the sand, snipped the Puffin's backside with its claws as hardly as it could, for one taunt deserves a capital jaunt. The Puffin gave a cry of pain, with a half throbbingly shrewd smile, and lurched high into the air.

The Puffin came diving down straight onto and through the Swan's neck, which hooked and crooked with great pain and swooped into and through the deep water. The Puffin popped out with one fluid motion, a Tattler on each shoulder. Immediately the Tattlers jumped from its shoulders and ran off, pursued by the Tattletailers, the Crab who might be thought to be a Lobster, the Lemmings tied by blue lace, and the Baboon, who was a Baboon as far as all were now concerned. The Puffin remained, as did its new found love of the water, watching the Swan struggle, flapping its wings and feet, with its neck bent right out of shape.

WHY THE COW TOOK A FLY
SWAT FOR A TAIL

Mysteries and phenomena are often tough to explain. What can be
a treacherous problem for some might be a rather simple one for
others. If you say, ask someone of religious belief and someone of
academically scientific prowess to explain the same mystery, they
will both come up with definite yet different answers. However, such
answers, whether Genesisian or Darwinian, are usually too general
to explain anything specific, such as the mysteries of how to open
medicine bottles, of why if you run in the rain you still get wet,
and of cows. There are many puzzling things to the Cow, from the
reasoning behind it having black splotches on its sides and back to its
'moo', which is in fact a human misconception, as so many mysteries
are, as the Cow is actually calling out 'moon', an entirely understand-
able behaviour if you know the whole story. So while on the point,
I happen to know the whole story and nothing but the story, so hail
me the stage, and I'll tell you it, just so, in truth.

This tale is more less believable than others perhaps until you accept that phenomena are rather inexplicable by nature. At the birth of such phenomena, there were no overlying principles to be found, and none under either. Sophisticated names were given, and conceptions were formed to match those names so that teachers had something to teach, and physicists something to physic, but when natural laws govern, they cannot be told how to behave. At this time also, each animal was finding its place within these laws and figuring their habits so as to abide by them, for breaking a law even then was inadvisable, making it very difficult to find occupations of any nature. The Little Dog chose to chase its tail, the Bee chose to buzz, though why and the manner with which it achieved this is another story altogether, and the Cow selected to have udders.

The Cow's logic went something like this – milk tastes good. The Cow was also partial to yoghurt, cream, and especially cheese, so it really was a wise choice. Possibly because the Cow itself was pure white, or possibly because it had no tail, though possibly not, the Cow made pail after pail of pale white milk, which it drank happily and sold at organic markets or gave away in exchange for bases to eat its cheese with. The Cow ate its cheese with grapes and strawberries, with a big fish, with basil pasta and rye bread, with anything and everything it could in fact. The Cow became quite absorbed in finding new ways to eat its cheese, to which end the Cow left its home where it had been born and calved, to find as many new recipes as it could, even those that lead to disasters, as a cheese disaster is the most delicious kind to clean up.

The Cow first arrived at a coffee shop atop a hill, where the Proprietor, with undoubtedly odd speaking manners, suggested trying the cheese with coffee and perhaps an egg to 'eggstract the flavourings', which the Cow tried and indeed thought very good, before moving on its way.

The Cow wandered incontestably straight into the forest, in which the Monkey lived, and the woods, in which the Fox lived, which were, in fact, the same treed area though neither of them knew it. Despite this linguistic miscommunication, the Fox and Monkey were great friends, although it did mean when planning to meet they instead discovered themselves in quite different locations regularly, but it happened on this occasion that the Cow had encountered the two when they had also encountered each other and were presently making a fire. The Monkey was gathering pieces of dry forest while the Fox was clapping clapping rocks to make a spark.

As the Cow approached, both looked up and, being incredibly friendly and immeasurably kind, without even an introduction, spoke to the Cow as one spoke to an old friend who one had expected to see were one to be where one was.

'You came,' said the Monkey. 'Be a deer and stack the fire will you.' The Cow could not fathom how a deer stacked a fire, but it tried to occasionally buck and make deer-like bleats and grunts that came out something more like that of an ambulance siren, as that was what it imagined a deer might do.

'Wonderful. Now stick it.'

'Stick what?' the Cow asked, entirely lost.

'The fire, of course.'

'Stick the fire,' the Cow said softly to itself. 'With what?'

'Don't worry deer, I'll do it,' said the Fox, placing some sticks on the fire. 'Now could you leave it?' So the Cow backed away a few steps, lowering its head a little to show it was complying.

'How're you to leave it from over there? Don't worry deer, I'll do it,' said the Monkey, placing a handful of leaves on the fire and sitting down around their quite impressive accomplishment.

'So what can we do for you deer?' inquired the Fox, looking up.

'Well,' the Cow began, 'I am searching for new recipes and ways to eat my delicious cheese. I'd be ever so glad to exchange a pail of this milk for any recipes you have to share,' it offered, voice raising a little higher in pitch so that it was clearly excited by the thought of learning a somewhat new recipe.

'Then I have just the thing for you,' the Monkey jumped up saying and ran off into the forest, leaving the other two to sit and speak of other things. When the Monkey returned, it was carrying bundles of fruit – stacks of grapes in one hand and piles of strawberries in the other.

'I'm sure with these your cheese will be magnificent deer,' said the Monkey gladly.

'I'm sure you are udderly correct,' the Cow said with a wink and a nudge and with clearly some of the coffee shop Proprietor still in its mind, 'but actually, I've tried the cheese with grapes and strawberries, and it is indeed delicious but not new.'

'Then I have the thing for you,' the Fox sprung up saying, with a little harder stress on the 'I' and ran off into the wood, leaving the other two to sit and talk on other topics. When the Fox came back, it had a big fish hanging from its mouth.

'I'm sure with this your cheese will be superb deer,' said the Fox cheerily.

'I'm sure you are not mistaken, but as with the fruit,' the Cow looked down a little disappointed, though fully aware it was not the fault of the Monkey or the Fox, 'I have tried my cheese with a big fish already, so it is not new either.'

'Hold on a second,' said the Monkey.

'Just wait a moment,' agreed the Fox, leaving the Cow unsure whether it should be holding on to the second or not.

'Our good friend, the Rabbit, makes the most scrumptious rice cakes imaginable. In fact, they're almost unimaginable. Just try to imagine your cheese with them. I guarantee it will be difficult.'

The Cow tried as it might, but, not having tried the scrumptious rice cakes before, it couldn't. So hearing this news, the Cow would have started wagging its tail left and right had it had a tail to wag.

'But alas, our good friend the Rabbit recently moved to live with the Old-man-of-the-moon and make scrumptious rice cakes up there. I'm afraid the only way to go would be to fly.'

'Bother,' remarked the Cow. Had it only chosen flight instead of udders this wouldn't be a problem. Though, with phenomena still partially indefinite, anything was definitely conceivable.

'It is well known that the Reindeer flies once a year, so why shouldn't you fly today deer?' suggested the Fox, which was enough to convince even the stoutest of minds.

The Cow had never flown before, but it had also never bucked or bleated, so was pretty confident. Besides, it suredly could do anything were it to receive a new recipe. So fly the Cow would try.

It first bent its neck, then its back, then knees, ankles, and hooves, though it could not bring itself to bend its calves, as they were still so young and taking a deep breath, jumped up into the sky. On the way, it passed other jumping animals; it passed the forlorn looking Bee, who glided silently; it passed where Reindeers would come once a year, and it passed its jump altogether so that it realised it was actually flying. The Cow had reached a hop before it had even struck a skip and occasionally fumbled into a jump, but it had never hit a fly, and now it hit a fly with a splatter. The Fly splattered all over the Cow's sides, back and face, and even in the Cow's eyes. As a result, two equally distressing things happened. First, the Cow, not being able to see where it was going, went clear all the way over the moon, missing it entirely, and came right back down to the forest or wood from where it had jumped. The second being that on the way the Cow had dropped pail after pail of pale white milk and covered the moon entirely, which, with the churning of the Rabbit beating rice in its mortar, turned the moon's surface quickly into a layer of thick cheese, not to the Old-man-on-the-moon's dissatisfaction.

Now it was once noted to me, by a tier maker no less, that the last paragraph of this story covered a lot of ground in one leap, a comment which worked in so many ways, it must have entirely exhausted itself. But I digress.

'Whatever happened deer?' asked the Monkey. 'Why are you back so soon and covered in fly?' it continued as the Fox tried washing the marks off.

'Sorry deer,' said the Fox. 'This fly won't come off. You've got fly on top of you and on your sides but at least not down below you; it would be awfully embarrassing to be left with your fly down. Well, what'll you do now?'

'I must jump to the moon once more, but this time I must stay in a jump and avoid hitting a fly,' said the Cow resolutely sure of its next move, though not how it might be achieved. All three thought long and hard, that is, they spent a hard time coming up with long thoughts on the matter and came up with no soft conclusion. The Cow would need a fly swat.

The Monkey and the Fox, being as friendly and immeasurably kind as they were, both quickly got to their feet and ran off into the treed area that went by many names. The Monkey came back with a thick papaya fruit plant, with its single stalk and leaf-bush tip.

'I'm sure papaya is delicious with cheese; in fact, I know so,' started the Cow.

'No deer,' the Monkey replied plucking, peeling, and eating up half of the fruit, leaving the other half for the Fox. 'You can use the tree with its thick stalk and bushy end as a fly swat.'

The Fox then returned having caught a beautifully large Snake-mackerel-oilfish.

'I'm sure the Snake-mackerel-oilfish is divine with cheese, but alas, I know it to be true,' started the Cow sympathetically, trying to spare the Fox's feelings.

'No deer, don't be a goose,' the Fox said back while wringing the fish, biting it into two and placing the two halves on the fire, one for the Fox and one for the Monkey.

'The waxy oil wrung from this fish can make any stiff branch or stalk into a supple, swingable twine, perfect for fly swatting.'

So the Cow, of course thanking the two, pruned and oiled the papaya stalk into a perfect fly swat. However, fly swat having been made, the Cow realised it had nowhere to hold it with, as, with neck bent, back bent, and knees, ankles, and hooves all bent, ready to jump, they could not also be expected to hold the swat.

'Put it in your rump deer,' said the cheeky Monkey, with hands dripping with fish oil.

'Yes, your rump is tender enough to hold it,' said the equally cheeky Fox, with mouth covered in papaya juice. The Cow thought this an excellent idea, also considering it had no tail yet where the other two both had one.

With the fly swat in its rump, the Cow once more bent its entire body and sprung itself into the air. It passed all manner of things on the way up, but as it struck and passed a jump and came to hit a fly, its new-found tail swung left and swatted the pesky fly right out of the way, and the Cow landed directly on the moon, besides the Rabbit, who was still busy at work. Having heard the Cow's story thus far, which went much like the story I have thus far told except not including this sentence, the Rabbit, being the friendliest and kindest of them all, at least to an extent that made it just a little strange, offered the Cow to come back to the grove, by which it meant the treed area where it believed it used to play with its two friends and to hop onto the fire so that the Cow could try cheese with the Rabbit. This offer, although sounding surprisingly tasty, was quite unsound, and the Cow politely and simply said that it would make do with taking some of the Rabbit's scrumptious rice crackers instead, the Rabbit permitting. Gladly permitting, especially considering that it now had a cheese moon to share with the Old-man-on-the-moon-who-lived-there-also, the Rabbit gave generously.

The Cow returned to the treed area of innumerable names and the fireplace of the Monkey and the Fox, and the three together tried rice crackers and cheese, which was indeed a rare delicacy of light flavours, not fighting but perfectly complimenting each other, as they were all equally friendly and kind.

WHY THE RABBIT HAS
DANDELION EARS

Some animals have long hanging ears; some have stubbed rounder ears, and some have no sign of ears at all, but don't let them fool you; one thing is for certain – all have reasons for having ears. The Elephant has ears to fan and cool itself in the hot months, and the Fennec Fox has ears in order to look adorable, or perhaps that is simply what happened to happen when it got the ears, and the Cock has ears in order to hear. The true question is, why does the Rabbit have such soft and standing ears? This is a tougher, true question than many and could well stump most. If you did, say, ask your mother, who may or may not have already tried to explain the Peacock and its tail, you might be told something along the lines of the ears being, much like the Fennec Fox's, 'so cute', and then you may have received a big bear hug, which, though usually appreciated, you felt was inappropriate at your time of academic investigation. The truth is, your mother knows a lot more than many, for reasons that stump most, but she doesn't know this because no one does, other than the Rabbit itself and I. So I shall give the real account of why the Rabbit has such soft, standing ears here, just so, in truth.

In weathers that permitted peeping into unillustrated books and the consideration, though not making thereof, of the worthiness of making a daisy-chain, animals run usually unnoticed around their dens and burrows, finding themselves for whatever reason on time for everything, possibly because there is very little that required them being strictly on time for. This story begins here between these dens and burrows and long sun-kissed grasses broken only by the twisting roots of hollow, though not disused, trees, and with two fallacies supporting each other like two sleeping children leaning back to back until one nods off forward, leaving the other now unsupported to topple back and over the first. It is, at least here, inaccurate, in that it is in the range of accuracy though has not quite hit the mark, or else it would be onaccurate to say that the Rabbit was entirely white with long standing ears or to assume that any animal late, with ears or without, is late to meet the Queen. So in this weather, between the dens and burrows, rushed earlessly late for a date, though not with the Queen, the White Rabbit, though with paws by then more a dusty brown.

The White Rabbit was a character of general punctuality, or else it would have never been heralded for its daytime position of working for the Queen. At night, the Rabbit returned to the moon, where it pounded mochi rice, but that's another story possibly already told. And in order to keep punctual, the White Rabbit saved pieces of time for when they were most needed, it kept a timepiece. This particular timepiece looked far like a clock kept in the pocket to which it was attached by a chain but by far was not a pocket-watch. Though the two looked similar, a pocket-watch tended to have a fob to its chain where hung a small winding key as time had to be prepared to keep up, whereas a timepiece had none, as a timepiece did not so much watch time, as it did nest a finite amount in reserve.

That day the White Rabbit had let its hot morning daze continue longer than it would normally, lying on tough red-tipped Blanket flowers and looking at the Moonbeams in the partial shade, which, although they preferred sunny spots, were taking a rest from the competition. The White Rabbit rose to dust pollen and dangler off its waistcoat jacket, as it had a very important date to go to, and took its timepiece from its inner pocket. An extra hour, it thought, would be enough. It had saved plenty, after all. But when it tried to use its time carefully, the White Rabbit noticed that it had all been spent, a revelation that sent the White Rabbit into a bit of a tizz, followed by a moment of fluster. There was no time left to visit the Watchmaker, this timepiece looking far like a pocket-watch but not being one was made by the Keeper who currently lived with the Watchmaker, a very confusing set up for sure, but there you are. And considering the White Rabbit had a few other errands to walk, it instead hopped off on a run, which no doubt deserves an expression of its own.

The White Rabbit's first call was to the Umbrella Whittler and Inspector to pick up its order of one repaired umbrella, as the White Rabbit had torn the canopy of its umbrella, when riding it, overturned, down the Floret Hill in order to avoid the blue laces or yellow buttons, as it didn't want to be a crotchet for it wasn't all too musical, discarding its prowess at blowing a trumpet, but for that it only knew only one or two notes really, and it didn't want to be a catch either as it particularly disliked puzzles and couldn't bear conundrums. But entering under the hanging clackety wooden sign engraved with the Umbrella Whittler's and Inspector's names – 'The Umbrella Whittler and Inspector's' – there was neither an Umbrella Whittler nor Inspector to be seen. What there was, was a lot of pictures of aquatic birds and dabbling drakes, which seemed more than awry to the White Rabbit.

'Fine morning,' the White Rabbit called, pausing for a reply. 'I say.

Fine morning. Are you by chance done with my umbrella? Only, I have a very important date to be getting to.' But no reply came whatsoever, other than the agreeable clacking of the hanging sign outside.

'Psst,' the White Rabbit heard, 'Psst,' from behind the hard counter. And up popped a small wooden head. The head swayed back and forth pssting until the White Rabbit had no choice but to clasp it, one hand to each cheek, and force it focus its hollowed acrylic eyes. 'Why, you are a duck's head!' said the White Rabbit, confused that the Duck's head should be pssting so calmly with it being clasped by the Rabbit, as they dislike anything but roses being put to their cheeks.

'Psst, it's done,' quivered the Duck's head between its palms. 'What's done?' whispered the White Rabbit, leaning in. The White Rabbit, in fact, leant in far enough, though not intentionally so, to see somewhat behind the hard counter, where sat crouching the Umbrella Whittler and Inspector, holding the foot of an umbrella, to which the head was clasped in the White Rabbit's hands.

'Why are you hiding down there?' queried the White Rabbit. 'And do you mean to tell me that this fellow', it indicated the wooden fowl it clasped, 'is my umbrella?'

'We aren't hiding; we are ducking.'

'What are you ducking from?'

'What are we what? No, we are ducking and have been all day,' with which the Umbrella Whittler gesticulated about the carving tools and carving flakes and carved carvings all of aquatic birds and dabbling drakes.

'I see. And why have you been ducking all day?' the White Rabbit asked, not removing its hands from the wooden head or moving at all rather.

'Just yesterday I was abruptly called a quack, and ever since that blasted sign out there has been reminding me.' The White Rabbit looked outside to see nothing in particular.

'I think that sign may be clacking rather than quacking,' the White Rabbit began, but it was no use, as neither the Umbrella Whittler nor the Inspector was listening.

'And if it quacks like a duck, then it's a duck, but if it's a duck, and

I'm a quack…' the White Rabbit began to back away slowly, as it seemed the explanation would take a while, and it had no whiles to give.

As the White Rabbit left under the hanging clackety wooden sign, it could still hear a faint jabbering from behind the hard counter. It had not intended to have its umbrella ducked, and holding it at the shaft meant gripping its neck, which would quite suffocate the fellow, but since it didn't mind being clasped at the cheeks, perhaps also didn't mind a soft smothering.

'I've not seen you in my neck of the woods before, are you heading my way?' chuckled the White Rabbit, who was not well-known for its edgy humour but liked to crack jokes now and then, though unfortunately often cracked beyond repair. 'My dear,' it mumbled, 'I am now getting quite late for that important date.'

The White Rabbit's final errand was to pick something up, and it had to be a good something, as it was to be a gift on the date, but with all whiles run out and all moments left with them, there wasn't a moment to lose, so instead of going to Ms. Primrose Pumpernickle's botanical bakery, the White Rabbit decided some wild growing flowers would be suitably light. In the field through which the White Rabbit was already hopping roamed, as it seemed, the Nipponjika had not yet been here to eat them all up, countless wild dandelions. So the White Rabbit picked up a few. Unfortunately, the White Rabbit had no more than two arms with two hands at each end, and in one was its repaired and ducked umbrella, while in the other its timepiece, so the White Rabbit topple-plumped itself down, brushing its waistcoat jacket back so not to also pick up dust, pollen, or dander, and it being the weather for it, began to tie a dandelion-chain. With the dandelion-chain done, the White Rabbit plump-popped it on its head and hopped up and off again, every now and then stopping to

check the timepiece and work itself into a ruffle.

Running between dens and burrows, the White Rabbit searched for its hole, but with the dandelion-chain constantly falling over its eyes it became hazardous, to say the least. Seeing this and knowing the impending important date, down fluttered the Butterfly.

'Follow me, White Rabbit. I'll be your eyes. We can't have you being late now.'

'Oh, thank you. It's the darndest thing, but I can't see for the life of me,' with which he followed aft the Butterfly so as the Butterfly bobbed left or right, so did the White Rabbit. The Butterfly indeed bobbed left and right and around trees and over logs, and so did its little white tail, and as it did, the dandelion stalks and leaves upon its head wiped over trees and logs picking up the sap and getting all sticky, while at the same time exciting the dandelion blowball tops. Had the White Rabbit then known that the blowball tops were also known as clocks, for blowing on them would pick up the finely haired seeds in a wind, winding them back to reset the clock head, which would have given the White Rabbit as much time as puffs it had in its chest, it would have been well enough. Alas, the White Rabbit had not learnt this yet, and so let the finely haired seeds waft up and off, as it bobbed. But most of the seeds did not waft off at all – they stuck fast to the sticky sap on the stalks and leaves over the White Rabbit's head.

The Butterfly and the White Rabbit bobbed past the Squirrel up its tree, past the Chameleon on a rock, though all it could see was the rock, past a dainty blonde-haired girl, who may or may not have followed it for no apparent reason other than curiosity and, thanking the Butterfly, down its White Rabbit hole. Down its White Rabbit hole, through its pantry and out through its White Rabbit sized door, the White Rabbit, though with paws now a deep muddy brown, bobbed. Finally, the White Rabbit arrived at the doghouse, not without time but in time for a disparaging nag. All there, tails wagging and snouts dripping, they were. Three quarters through the fifth verse of the ceremonial five-verse song, and as they ended, the White Rabbit stepped forward.

'Forgive my being late,' said the White Rabbit, bobbing its head independent from its body.

'I know this important date marks the start of the dog days.'

'Si, si,' jumped up the small black-faced Pug, tongue inexplicably hanging out of the top of its mouth.

'Has you bring us'es presents? Presents!' it panted repeatedly and quickly, while running in circles, apparently hungry enough to eat its own tail.

'I have these wild dandelions,' said the White Rabbit, reaching to its head but finding two white, long, standing, and finely haired ears instead.

Why the rabbit has dandelion ears   **181**

'Ah, well, how about a game?'

A game perhaps of Tweedlywinks it thought but had none of the appropriate pieces and concluded that the dogs, were they to get any more excited, would be knocking pieces this way and that with wagging tails had they the pieces anyway. Finally, the White Rabbit placed its timepiece dangling from the wooden beak of its repaired, though ducked, umbrella, to swing around left and right. This seemed at first a poor excuse for a game, even if it were a gift, on such a very important date, but as it swung back and forth, a small thudding sound grew and grew as each tail in the room started to wag back and forth and beat against the floor.

After all the festivities, the White Rabbit, who by now was muddied and stained in all manner of ways, making it not white at all, returned home to rest its slightly heavier than usual head. Looking in its bedside mirror, the Rabbit stroked one of its soft and standing ears. 'These ears being much like the Fennec Fox's are indeed so cute. I think I'll keep them,' it may have mumbled, though it was rather hard to hear as the Rabbit drifted off to sleep.

Dog Days

The first two verses of the ceremonial five-verse song of the dog days were recounted to me once by a rather Cavalier King Charles Spaniel, so I have no reason to doubt them other than the fact that they were recounted rather unceremoniously. So were you to ask me to sing them for you, which I'm sure you were, they went something like this, though my voice can hardly do them justice...

'Hot, like kettles on an open stove, ya ya,
Hot, like windows closed in a car just drove
To the sea, which too is boiling hot enough to make your tea.

Hot, like chewing a stolen meatball, ya ya,
Hot, like wearing a thick cotton shawl
At the park, when chasing squirrels is keeping you busy.

Ooh, I can't find my mind, so

Gimme all your biscuits, or I will bite you, or so the stars say
Gimme all your biscuits, or I'll let you know that it's now the dog days.

Hot, as if your tail has caught alight, ya ya,
Hot, as if you've gone and got in a fight
With a cat who burned rubber and shot straight up a tree.

Hot, as if you drank coffee in one gulp, uh huh
Hot, as if you ate a whole light bulb
And it's burning bright; you can feel all of that light energy.

Ooh, I buried my last mind, so

Gimme all your biscuits, or I will bite you, or so the stars say
Gimme all your biscuits, or I'll let you know that it's now the dog days.'

WHY THE SHIBA DOG CURLED ITS TAIL

If you are in fact a cat lover, then this question may not have occurred to you, though now that it is out there, you perhaps have started to wonder it also. This question that has baffled dog lovers for a yonk and a half – why do some dogs' tails curl up? And, why does the apostrophe come after the 's'? The latter question is simple because there are so many dogs in case that the apostrophe cannot keep up with them, but this confounds the former question, as each dog's tail must have a tale of its own. If you decide to inquire about, you, I suppose, will find that as a matter of case, no one can explain why some dogs have curled tails, but that is because you, I suppose, will not have asked me. So if you would tolerate it, I will describe the occurrences that lead to one dog's tail curling, the Shiba Inu, just so, in truth.

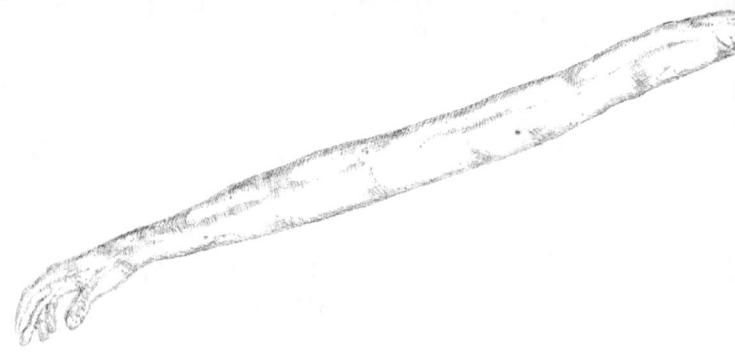

In the heart of Nippon, where Cranes perch one-legged in still
rock ponds beside moss covered granite lanterns, beneath the great
mountain that stands alone with snow covered top and sleeping fires
within that together heat the ground and cool the air, secluded and
cloistered within the field of blue trees so dense it blocks wind from
wisping through, so that the air sits calm and still, where it is so quiet
the soft dancing foot steps of the sprites of trees can be heard like
drops of water from a hanging cave drape that hit the cold floor and
echo a dousing impact around the walls, in here, where everything
is both dead and alive, or at least asleep and awake and indistin-
guishable, lived one of the first children of the first Seedsman, who
convinced by the pommnevorous dusky eve's presence had left his
garden to ruin. And here with the Child, lived as a companion and
friend, one of the first fourteen ancient breeds of dog, those being
the children of the wild wolves, the Shiba Inu.

The Shiba Inu, as with its thirteen blood cousins, was a pure breed. That being different to all later diluted breeds of dogs otherwise called muggles, whose blood ran thin having been mixed in small clay demitasse mugs, hence the name, in attempts to bear more superfluously desired traits such as longer legs or stouter noses. The Shiba Inu had natural traits almost lost in time, such as two coats of fur, which the Child called urajiro, meaning underwhite, for the undercoat was white as a snow leopards and had it only this undercoat it would truly resemble a wolf, and tsura-aka, meaning cheek red, for the thick surface coat of golden red, which covered the whole top of the Shiba Inu, leaving the urajiro exposed on its underside running from its jaw down its chest and across its belly.

The fourteen ancient breeds of dog, strong and savage as their feral kin but with the higher faculties of man, intelligence, and the appreciative power of will to preserve beautitude in its forms, watched over the Seedsman's gardens and children. They spread, as did the children, to diverse corners, from Siberia to Africa, rarely ever meeting again, though in this eastern island stretching long from the equatorial tropics to snowy tundra lived two of the fourteen, the Shiba Inu, and the eighth of the ancient breeds, the loyal, though aloof, Akita Inu, which denned in the mountainous north. The Shiba Inu was smaller than its northern cousin, which helped it navigate the dense field of blue trees. That, and one other characteristic, truly distinguished the Shiba Inu – its tail. The Akita Inu had a curled-up tail, in fact, all of the fourteen ancient breeds, except the Shiba Inu. Some, over time or trial, have flattened theirs down, and some held it down in meditative exercise to sharpen their senses, whilst the Akita Inu left it curled up with pride as a symbol of its pure breeding, but the Shiba Inu had no choice but to let it stay limp and low.

The truth is that not having a curled tail didn't bother the Shiba Inu much. If we think about it, we aren't bothered about our lack of a curled tail either. And since the Shiba Inu almost never met its cousins, it was far from mind, so not a point of contention or even a point at all. But at this point, the Shiba Inu was about to witness by doing a set of events that would result in the curling of a tail, though I won't tell you whose or else it would ruin the surprise, and the Shiba Inu would be thankful for the unexpected twist.

Since the Seedsman left, a stew of odd creatures and fiendish demons took up in the field of blue trees. Brothers from distant countries, the Ashinaga, or long legs, and the Tenaga, or long arms – old-man-like men, one with stretched dangling arms that dragged and one with long spindly legs that clacked and rattled. These at first the Shiba Inu let be but eventually had to drive south, as they would not stop eating the Heikegani, face-stealing crabs that took the faces of dead spirits on their shells. The Heikeganis particularly wanted to try a man's face and so often sought the Child, which meant they too had to be driven back, but since this was simply their nature, the Shiba Inu left them in the rock pools of the rivers, running silently through the blue trees.

The Tsurube-otoshi, a lurking demon with a long burning nose that skulks in the blue treetops until an unwitting prey walks under when it drops a bucket from a wishing well to scoop up its dinner. This the Shiba Inu also let stay, as, if you simply paid a gold coin and wished aloud that it wouldn't eat you, the Tsurube-otoshi tipped you free from the bucket muttering curses and rustling away. And if you had no gold coins, a chess piece or a tweedlywink piece would do as the Tsurube-otoshi couldn't see very well for the flame at the end of its large nose.

Here also lived the Chouchin-obake, or paper lantern ghost, formed of a bamboo frame and paper sides. It floated the dense field mouth open and elongated tongue hung loose. A hapless harmless demon that in fact was quite useful bringing light on dark nights.

However, in the field of blue trees, there also crept the Hikeshibaba, an old wrinkled woman with straggly hair and bent fingers and back that prowled around at night blowing out the lights of lanterns. The Hikeshibaba was a real wicked demon, for, in such a thickly treed field that spanned across the sun-blocked enclosure, light was more valuable than gold or even than chess or tweedlywink pieces. In fact, the Child occasionally fed the Chouchin-obake little wax pellets collected from the blue trees and little strands of wick to encourage it to stay. So the Shiba Inu became known within the fields of blue trees and without as the protector of light, and the Hikeshibaba was its infliction.

The Child and the Shiba Inu often went hunting for the Hikeshib-aba. The Child, still being too young in the growth of man to carry anything too sharp when running, ran instead with a slingshot and bag of dango, homemade sticky rice balls covered with sweet bean paste prepared especially for the old eyes of the Hikeshibaba. If the kuraphilic, or darkness-loving, Hikeshibaba were to finally blow

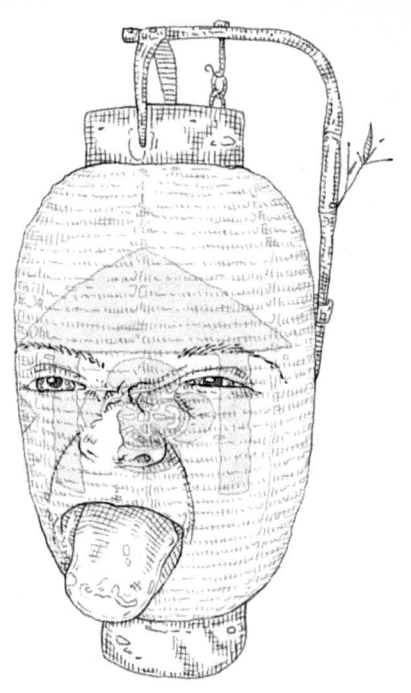

out all light, the field of blue trees would no longer be blue as colour would stop being, and what was indistinguishably asleep and awake would inevitably suffocate in a never-ending dream and the soft stillness would become dank dullness, which no creature or fiendish demon could stand or even sit in. However, if the Child could hit its mark, then only the Hikeshibaba's world would have the lights put out, which we can only assume it desired anyway. But in the unmoving muffle of the trees, the Hikeshibaba moved, being as light as old women, without footsteps.

The Child laid traps throughout the blue trees and left lucent candles in granite moss covered lanterns beside the still rock ponds and hidden between towering trees with small stone statues no bigger than a grown hand caped in red handkerchiefs to watch over them. The Child then sat in seiza, the proper seated position, with legs folded under knees, in the middle. Each luminant stone glowed dimly around the Child, next to who sat the Shiba Inu, also in seiza, having taught the Child unwittingly through demonstration and then learnt from the Child retrospectively by observation. The Shiba Inu leant back, ears pricked, sniffing the air. Suddenly to the left, one of the granite lanterns standing atop a great fallen trunk disappeared. Then the next and the one after that. As the lights went out in a dark enclosing circle around the two sitters, they stood to their knees, both focusing directly at what would be the last in the circle, which as each other light vanished appeared to get brighter and brighter by contrast. The Shiba Inu's teeth born and low gurgling sound vibrating from its throat, the Child, sling in hand and shot pulled back tense, awaited. The Hikeshibaba's old goblin face appeared from the dark mist contorted and shone in the lantern's glow. The Shiba Inu let out, though quite intentionally, a blood-thickening growl from its chest where it kept many such things and leapt forward as the Child, shot stretched back to its winced left eye, released the sticky dango just as the light vanished. But in the dark the Child could only see blackness, assuming blackness is a thing of sight, and the Shiba Inu, whose wolf eyes shine in the night, could see but had nothing but its fierce claws and teeth with which to use and did not want to hurt the devilish old hag, so when the Child had relit the granite lantern, the dango sat dripping on its side with a small tree sprite and the small Nettle Weevil licking the sweet bean paste and no sign of the Hikeshibaba.

The following evening, the two comrades set up the granite moss covered lanterns in much the same way and sat as they had the night before. Sitting beside each other in seiza they waited, breath held so as to make no sound and bulging their cheeks and in effect their eyes to help them see better, and sure enough, the lantern glows began to go dim around them. This time as the second to last light was eaten by the darkness, the Shiba Inu bound forward snarling through its teeth and barked a gruff clear bark, and the Child pointed the sling to the sound that signalled the approaching Hikeshibaba, but with the close-knit trunks of blue bark, the sound could be heard everywhere and rather melancholic, echoing, and moving around so that once again, when the final lantern was relit, there lay the dango with the same small tree sprite, the same small Nettle Weevil, and the Dead Nettle Leaf Beetle, all licking at the sweet bean paste.

On the third night, all laid out as the nights before, the moon shone bright and full, with the Rabbit and Old-man-who-lived-there watching down having smelt the sweet bean dangos but not seeing anything through the field of blue trees within which the Child and Shiba Inu sat hearing their own hearts beat slow and steady, when forthwith the left side gleam died as did each other in order. When the second to last was also flushed out, the Shiba Inu leapt forward, bent its right legs, and kicked up, spinning around in the air. With this twisting movement in an otherwise unbent and untouched scene, the floating sky upturned, left the Shiba Inu's tail in a circular shape, which focused on the final granite moss covered lantern, funnelling its rays of light as a spotlight framing the foul hag as she leaned in lips pressed. The Child let fly the dango, which whisked through the Shiba Inu's circular tail, guiding it like far-sight straight into the Hikeshibaba's left eye, forcing the crone to stumble back. Landing, the Shiba Inu bowed its left legs and again flung itself into the air, twisting around forcing the whole atmosphere around to open its eyes and roll out of its slumber, swirling the Shiba Inu's tail even further. Again the Child focused, shot aimed right to the old cow's eye, but then leaving the Cow alone for it had done nothing other than asking about dango and cheese, aimed back at the Hikeshibaba's final good, as in it worked and not as in it held any good moral aptitude, eye through the dogs fluffy frame and released. The dango whizzed through the tail making the air around pull each hair fluttering in its wake and hit the Hikeshibaba directly in its right eye, who coincidentally cowered back and stumbled over.

Soon, from behind the blue trees in the blackness emerged all sorts of onlookers – the Chouchin-obake slid hesitantly to the wicked hag, who, not being able to see its light, croaked at it to help support her to her feet. The same small tree sprite, the same small Nettle Weevil, the same Dead Nettle Leaf Beetle, and now the Eastern Grape Rootworm, all sat under the last light looking down at the tamed shrew and up at the Child, who placed one sweet bean paste dango in front of each. The Child made for home with the Hikeshibaba, who now was just a wrinkled old lady and might be able to help mix sweet bean paste with her bent fingers and pick rice with her bent back, with the Chouchin-obake lighting the way and with the Shiba Inu and its curled-up tail.

WHY THE TREE FROG HAS STICKY PADS ON ITS TOES

I like frogs. I like the Tree Frog especially, knowing what it has been through and its character in part. However, some people, it seems, dislike frogs. If you ask yourself whether you like frogs or not and come to the same conclusion as me, then good for you, though it is always best to wait to hear the story of what someone has been through and their character in part before judging either way really. However, if you conclude that you don't like frogs, for whatever reason, permit me to interject. You can ask why frogs have blemishes, though wouldn't you after so long in the sun? Or you can ask why they are so wrinkly, though wouldn't you be after so long in the water? You could even ask why the Tree Frog has sticky pads on its feet, which is, in fact, a very intelligent question to ask. There are good and bad everything, and anything can be difficult to truly understand, so nothing should be decided before you ask into it a little, for some things have very good reasons behind them. So, it is my turn to ask you to listen to the reasons behind them, as I would like to explain why the Tree Frog has sticky pads on its feet, just so, in truth.

When nature itself yawned and stretched out its arms with a gaphaw, and all life spread far and wide leaving no rock unturned or patch unthriving, teeming with the hurly-burly tumult of humour, not the funny but the kind of humour that seethes through the bodily fluids with energy and life, when this great expanse had ended, for the world is finite even if it is immeasurable, then there was only one way to go, up. So they climbed. The rocks climbed up into mountains, and the grasses climbed up into trees, and the animals climbed up the trees, though some, like the White Wolf, then realising their fear of heights climbed back down and feeling awfully abashed, especially when comparing themselves to others, like the White Leopard, fled to the cold tundra of the north to become the Arctic Wolf, though followed by what was then the newly endowed Snow Leopard, who went just to rub some faces in it.

Why the tree frog has sticky pads on its toes **199**

Tremend after tremend, the rising continued at an unfathomable degree, in fact so much so that no word other than tremendous would describe it, which was a rather new word then and so eager to make its mark. As did the animals inasmuch as climbing lofty trees inevitably left marks. The former White Leopard left claw marks running up the bark, while insects like the slug left lines of gloppity-gook trailing behind them, for whether with sharp grapplers on their paws or mucus-secreting pores on their bellies, a method to the madness of their scaling was required.

Amongst all this in the leafy undergrowth chirped the Tree Frog. The Tree Frog, not named for its ability to climb or be usually found in trees, was in fact named due to its colour being a deluxe green but mostly because its chirp sounded a lot like it was saying 'treee, treee'. This was quite unlike the digging and burrowing Purple Frog, named not because it was purple, as it was clearly a slightly dark mauve, but because its croak sounded like 'purr-ple, purr-ple'. The Tree Frog quite simply could not dig, burrow, or climb trees because it had no claws or sticky mucus with which to ascend. In fact, it could do very little other than sit chirping about trees and, being h'arboreal, at least in the western continent, harbouring realities to tell the most fascinating stories.

The Tree Frog told the story of L'Arbre du Ténéré, a tree so isolated and unaccompanied that even the desert sand around where it sat left a foot between itself and the tree so that the L'Arbre du Ténéré balanced its secluded trunk on nothing but that one foot. And the story of the Major's Oak, a burly oak one thousand years old, which with its clambering branches and clouded pockets housed one thousand heisters, scroungers, and merry marauders that burnt lamps and fires, singing into the night.

A break, as the Tree Frog keenly used, to create anticipation.

The Tree Frog's stories were so captivating in fact that the animals passing, whether heading past, around, or up the staple bases where it chirped, were hooked back, lined up, and sunk down to listen.

'Your stories are marvellous and miraculous, of that there is no question,' called one member of the audience snagged on a large treble hook. 'Each so full of fabule, one might even call them fabulous if so inclined and immune to the preposter of the word. But how are we to listen and head past, around or up our trees?' This was indeed true, as the Tree Frog orated its epic anecdotes as did the poets of old, with its voice, and a lot of hand gestures. The Tree Frog did not, however, record any of its saga for audiences to take with them and read on their journeys. Being an animal that preferred to gladden than pester, this concerned the Tree Frog dearly.

The Tree Frog first found a conch and asked for its shell, which it thought would make a brilliant loudspeaker. The Tree Frog was absolutely correct, but when its audience started to walk past, around, or up their respective trees, they could hear nothing but the sea, which wasn't unpleasant at all but peculiar considering where they were, and not much like a good story, so they concluded the conch was broken, and the Tree Frog gave it up.

The Tree Frog then went just down past the rising Cranberry bush and left at one of the famous Moon trees that, as a seed was obsessed with the astrological and finally visiting, found the lunar diet of cheese and rice humbly satisfying and of which the Tree Frog also narrated to the bookbinders. Having been asked by the bookbinder what it could be done for, the Tree Frog recounted its problem, recited its stories into a voluminous run-down, and returned to its staple base to chirp. So given the bound run-down, the audience tried to head past, around, or up their trees, reading, but it being so big being the least of their problems, and it always running back down the

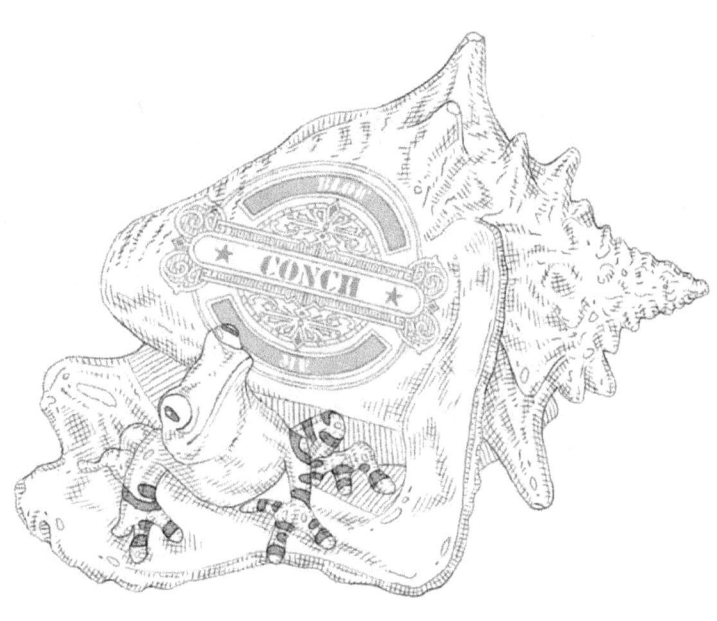

trees being the most of their problems, it too had to be given up.

'Give me a few days,' chirped the Tree Frog to its captivated audience. 'Return after your tea-time scones on the day of the week,' which some considered a national holiday in some parts, such as from five o'clock onwards, but saying it were a national holievening was a mouthful, 'and I'll be prepared. If not I'll eat that,' it pointed at a mushroom cap they all knew to be either poisonous or to have a bit of a kick to it and so were satisfied with the guarantee and left.

The Tree Frog thought and thought and brainstormed until it was red inside its face, which explains why some descendants of the Tree Frog now have red eyes popping out of their tree-coloured heads, and finally, the storm calmed, and the Tree Frog stood with brainclarity. Tearing each page from the now run-down volumes and some seawater and clinging kelp from inside the conch, the Tree Frog made a sticky notepad. If the trees were covered up with each page of its stories, then the audiences could climb and read at ease as they went, and how perfect that would be. So the Tree Frog fixed to make it so. Nonetheless howbeit notwithstanding the Tree Frog's sharp ideas and steadfast motives, it still had no claws or mucus with which to scale the trees and lay notes, but this would not stop such an ingenuous critter as it was.

The Tree Frog started at its staple base, pasting on the first few pages of its stories. It then used the clinging kelp on the pages, as they stuck to its toes, to support its modest weight on the tree before it started to paste the second few pages. The Tree Frog continued this process, with each tier in the ascent getting easier and peasier, to the top whereupon it conveniently ran out of pages. From the top, the Tree Frog looked down and thought two very distinct thoughts that stood quite clearly out, though remained quite clearly in its mind. The first thought was that this was the highest the Tree Frog had ever been, which was both scarily exhilarating and exhilaratingly scary. And the second thought was that it would be hard for its audiences to read all the pages of its stories as they climbed because they were all now stuck in little clumps on its toes, leaving none of the pasted pages on the tree at all.

So when the day of the week came, and all the audience had had their tea-time scones, some putting clotted cream first and raspberry jam second, while others spreading raspberry jam first and clotted cream second, but that's another sticky story, they all arrived to find no Tree Frog there at all.

'Where is the Tree Frog?' they asked each other redundantly. 'Wait, be quiet. Can you hear that chirp?' They all looked around for a moment to judge from where the chirp was coming and slowly come to the same conclusion, bending their necks back and raising their eyes. 'What are you doing up there?' they called, knowing the Tree Frog had no claws or mucus with which to scale trees.

'I have inadvertently glued note paper to my feet and now have a sticky pad on the end of each toe,' the chirp replied.

'Well, then how are you to tell us your stories?' called the audience, a little agitated by the stupend of the Tree Frog's current location, the stupend of the Tree Frog's still bloodshot eyes, and the stupend of what had lead to both of these occurrences, resulting in a stupendous spectacle.

'Well,' said the Tree Frog, taking a few steps down the tree, 'I suppose I could post it to you.'

'Post it? But how will we receive the post on our journeys?' the audience rightly pointed out. 'What's more, how are you to post it when it is now posted to your feet? Surely nothing as sticky and small as the pads on the tips of your toes now could be posted.'

'Ah,' the Tree Frog took a few more steps down while thinking. 'I suppose you're right. What was I thinking? Post-it.' The Tree Frog stopped and looked down with a twinkle in its bloodshot eyes that only occurs with a great idea.

'If you get someone of note, I'll drop them a line, up which they can come, and I'll write my stories upon them. Mind only if they are of note, or else I'll have nothing to say.'

'Yes,' the audience nodded, 'then they can come on our journeys, and we can read them like a book.'

'But wait,' interjected the Tree Frog, 'the only thing of true note around here is the Paper Mulberry, with its milk loving catkins, but it recently seems to go by Tapa Cloth Tree, which would be much harder to write on.' The Tree Frog finished, scratching its chin now leaning back on the staple base, as it had climbed all the way down to the bottom whilst talking.

'But now that you're here,' the Tree Frog leant forward, 'do you want to hear of the Arbol del Tule, or the Tree of Tule, a thirsty tree with a stoutly gnarled trunk in which, if you look close enough, you can see the faces of definite moments of note, such as when the Elephant helped the mischievous Mouse-deer from its pit, and from those pits and cracks in the misshapen knotted trunk, you can see the puffs of mist and cloud that make the Tule fogs?' As the Tree Frog told the story, the audience was listening intensely and heading past, around and up their trees, but the story didn't end until they realised they were all at the tops.

Now that the Tree Frog had sticky pads on its toes, it could climb the trees as well, and being a frog that had no appetite for its siblings, never got another frog in its throat and kept on telling its stories while walking up and down each sturdy tree trunk.

The pleasure's partly mine.

www.ingramcontent.com/pod-product-compliance
Lightning Source LLC
Chambersburg PA
CBHW060640260626
47161CB00008B/2927